The five young people from *Urban Heroes* face new challenges.

Gavin -- has just got his professional contract. Can he stand the pressure of being the star of the Youth team.

Shane -- has joined London Albion. Will he survive in the competitive atmosphere of a top English club?

El is still torn between athletics and soccer. No must a final choice.

L pigeons are still his consuming passion. He nurses secret ambition that can bring him into the big-t

Ja Scorpion Jake is on the up and up. But vital decisions must be made. Where does the future of the b lie?

PETER REGAN writes from personal experience. He once managed a schoolboy team, and as 'Chick' Regan masterminded the Avon Glens and Brighton Celtic. Today he is a spectator, following the fortunes of Liverpool and Glasgow Celtic.

Born in Keadue in north Roscommon, he now lives in where he runs a small fuel and seed business. This explains his interest in and his knowledge of the pigeon-racing scene.

Going for Glory moves from London to Greystones, from Dublin to Belfast. It is humorous, highly entertaining, but with a cutting edge. Peter Regan's ear and eye for the nuances of the youth scene are as sure as ever.

Other books by Peter Regan: *Urban Heroes*, *Touchstone*, *Revenge of the Wizards*.

Peter Regan

TEEN GLORY

Illustrated by Terry Myler

THE CHILDREN'S PRESS

All characters are fictional.
Any resemblance to real persons, living or dead,
is purely coincidental.

First published 1993 by
The Children's Press
an imprint of Anvil Books
45 Palmerston Road, Dublin 6

4 6 5 3

ISBN 0 947962 78 6

Typeset by Computertype Limited
Printed by Colour Books Limited

Dedicated to
Jack Murnane

1

Gavin Byrne was about to become a professional footballer. In two days time he was due to go to the first-team manager's office and sign a professional contract. Not bad for a kid who had come over from Ireland a year previously as an apprentice. But Gavin Byrne was no ordinary footballer. He oozed class. London Albion, one of the top teams in the English FA Premiership, were only too glad to have him on the club's books. He was a certainty to make it into the big time. Two days time would be the eighth of August, Gavin's seventeenth birthday.

On the appointed day, when Gavin went to John Warner's office, the contract was on the desk. He didn't attempt to read it. He signed the document straight away.

All John Warner said was, 'It's a three-year contract. By London Albion standards, as good as any kid your age could get. We've a future for you, Gavin. Welcome on board.'

'Does that mean I get to play with the reserves?'

'Not yet. We're holding you back until your FA Youth Cup run is over. Then, maybe, we'll blood you.'

'That's great, Mr Warner. Just terrific.'

'Course it is . . . By the way, there's something up with Keith Jardine. Has he mentioned anything to you?'

'No.'

Keith Jardine was one of two apprentices who shared digs with Gavin. The other was Sandy Black. Keith was from Scotland, Sandy from Belfast.

'I've offered the lad a professional contract. He won't sign it.'

'Why not? Is he looking for better terms?'

'No. He said nothing like that. We think there's another club involved. Some club must have got at him during the summer. Gavin, could you try and find out who it is?'

'Mr Warner, I'm not doin' that. Keith's my mate. It's up to him to tell you if there's anythin' goin' on. I'm keepin' out of it.'

'Have it your way. But there must be another club involved. He wants to hold back. There has to be another club in there meddling.'

Gavin had a good idea who the other club was: Glasgow Rangers. But he didn't say anything. He kept his mouth shut.

'It's nothin' to do with me, Mr Warner.'

'Fair is fair, I suppose. Thanks for signing the contract straight off. You haven't let yourself down. And you're a club asset now. By the way, your friend from Ireland arrived about an hour ago.'

'Hammer?'

'Shane Teale.'

'Hammer's his nickname. Where's he stayin', Mr Warner?'

'With Keith, Sandy and yourself. He's at the digs now, waiting for you to finish up.'

Gavin felt great. He couldn't think straight. He was totally elated. London Albion thought the world of him. They had given him a professional contract. And his longtime friend Hammer was back at the digs, waiting to start out as an apprentice footballer with London Albion. It would be just like old times.

Gavin left the office in a daze – a professional footballer! In the words of John Warner, he was a club asset. He planned a quiet celebration with Hammer, Sandy and Keith.

It was some feeling.

Stevie Hodgson, the Youth-team manager, was waiting in

the corridor outside John Warner's office. He congratulated Gavin.

'A three-year contract?'

'Suits me fine.'

'Did the Boss say anything about Keith Jardine?'

'Not a lot. Anyway, it's none of my business.'

'Suppose you're right. Time will tell. I've a few minutes to spare. Let's get a quick cup of tea from Mrs Dawson.'

Mrs Dawson was the tea lady. The players and backroom staff were always dropping in to her for a quick cuppa and a consoling chat. She was more like a mother to them, especially the apprentices. Stevie Hodgson and Gavin didn't go into the main canteen area, but into the kitchen itself. Mrs Dawson, in the background, added her own views to what was being discussed: the composition of the Youth squad. The midfield area was sound, especially with Mick Bates, the 'Ealing Terror' as anchorman. In his last season at Youth level, he was the only other Youth on a professional contract apart from Gavin and Keith Jardine – that is if Keith accepted the offer.

And that was one problem for Stevie – one thorny problem.

'I'd hate to lose Keith. It'd upset the whole balance of the defence.'

Keith, who played left-full, was a polished performer. A real Scottish thoroughbred. Like Gavin, Hammer and Sandy Black, he still had two seasons left at Youth level before he would be overage.

'I'd hate to lose Keith,' repeated Stevie.

'Losin' Keith wouldn't be the end of the world. I know Sandy Black hit a bad patch last season, but he's back in form now. If Keith leaves, bring Sandy back in at right-full and move John Palmer to left-full in place of Keith. That leaves the team the same as last season except for Colin Baker in goal and Darren Blyth up front. And you've good replacements for them. Jeff Harker looks a better

9

goalkeeper than Colin. And Cyril Stevens can do a good job in attack. He may not be as good as Darren, but he's still good. Don't forget Cyril is an England Youth international.'

'Yeah, at centre-half, not centre-forward.'

'He's mobile, skilled, and he's a good shot.'

'You tryin' to tell me my job?'

'No, Stevie, only tryin' to help. Move Cyril to centre-forward and put Hammer centre-half.'

Stevie laughed. Told Gavin to drink up. That it was time to leave Brompton and go back to Highfield for a spot of training. Brompton was London Albion's home stadium. Highfield was their training grounds and the place where most of the South-East Counties League matches were played.

When Stevie Hodgson and Gavin got to Highfield the Youth Squad was already going through some circuit training under the direction of Bill Thornbull, the team trainer. The lads liked to call him the team bully, an expression that didn't enthuse him. He was a fitness fanatic. But underneath the hard exterior he wasn't the worst. The Youths were afraid of him though, more so than of Stevie. But Bill was a useful commodity to have around the Youth-team squad. Some of the players were giddy, and he was just the person to keep a tight rein. He was something of a trouble-shooter, a John Wayne of the playing fields.

Bill had started pre-season training by giving Sandy Black extra training on weights, lapping and sprinting. He was determined to have him out there on the starting-blocks to regain the right-full spot he had lost the season before. He knew that Keith Jardine was going to leave London Albion and John Palmer would be moved to fill the gap. That would leave the right-full position for Sandy, and Bill was determined to have him in top condition. Not only was Bill a good trainer. He had an excellent football

10

brain, especially as far as anticipation was concerned. And he could read kids inside out.

Gavin felt pleased about Hammer joining him at London Albion. Gavin and Hammer had started out together playing football in their home town, Greystones. They had played for the local schoolboy club, Shamrock Boys, below the railway embankment in Greystones. They had played together right up to U-14 level, when Gavin left and joined Cambridge Boys from Ringsend. From there Gavin had gone on to win Irish Schoolboy caps and to sign for London Albion. In the meantime, Hammer's team at Shamrock Boys had broken up and he had joined St Joseph's, Sallynoggin.

Gavin had left a lot of boyhood friends behind him when he signed for London Albion, mainly Hammer, Jake, who had a yen for playing the guitar and had his own pop-group, and Luke Doyle, a quiet sort who liked nothing better than spending his time looking after and racing pigeons. And there was Elaine Clarke. Elaine was an accomplished 800 metres runner and a fine footballer.

Unlike Gavin, Hammer felt full of apprehension about coming to London. Right at the last minute he felt like pulling out. Only that Gavin was already over in London he probably would have ducked the move. He felt worried and tense going over on the plane. Even worse, when the club representative met him at the airport and brought him to the digs, Gavin wasn't there. Neither were the other two, Sandy and Keith. They were still at training. Mrs Burtinshaw, the landlady, did her best to put Hammer at ease. Her house typified homeliness, right down to the grandfather clock in the hallway, and the cosy coal fires she fuelled during the winter.

It wasn't until Gavin came back to the digs with Sandy and Keith that Hammer began to unwind, especially when Gavin began to ask about what was happening back home.

'How's Jake?'

'Just great. Messin' as usual.'

'Luke?'

'Happy enough.'

'How's his pigeons doin', then?'

'Beginnin' to click. They're up near the top every race.'

'How's Elaine?'

'Runnin' all the time. Her season's just over. She's thinkin' of playing some football.'

'With Brighton Celtic?'

'Yeah.'

'How's Lar Holmes?'

Lar Holmes was Hammer and Gavin's ex-schoolboy manager at Shamrock Boys.

'Lar's keepin' great. He's thinkin' of startin' an U-12 team with Shamrock Boys. Your little brother says he'll play for him.'

'He didn't tell me that.'

'And Lar's got a job again – roadworking for the County Council.'

So far neither Keith nor Sandy had said a lot. They were quite content to just listen, especially Keith. He was cheesed off at training with nothing but query after query as to whether he was staying with the club or going back to Scotland.

'Gavin just signed as a professional today.'

'You did?'

'Yeah, the four of us are goin' out to celebrate soon as tea's over.'

'Think Mrs Burtinshaw'll let us?'

'Sure.'

It wasn't every day one of Mrs Burtinshaw's boys signed a professional contract as a footballer. She certainly wouldn't object to a night's celebration. Anyway, it was a once-off. The lads knew how to behave. They could be trusted.

'How come ye didn't get over for the start of pre-season trainin'?' Sandy asked Hammer. Sandy was a stickler for training.

'I had things to do at home . . . My sister was getting married . . . But she brought the wedding forward.'

'You close to your family?'

'Yeah.'

'Me too.'

Mrs Burtinshaw called them into the dining-room for tea.

'Homesick?' asked Sandy, sensing that Hammer was ill at ease.

'A little.'

Sandy sympathized. Then he waited for Mrs Burtinshaw to move out of earshot before continuing in a serious voice, 'This club's bigger than homesickness. I'd have nothin' back home, only trouble. This place gets me away from all that.'

'We don't wanna hear about life in Belfast,' protested Keith. 'There's enough about it on TV.'

Sometimes Keith got on Sandy's nerves. This was one such occasion. 'I'm only usin' what I'm goin' to say as an example for Hammer to grasp how lucky he is to get a chance with London Albion, and not to feel homesick.'

'You're not gonna tell him about when you were home for the summer a fella asked you to take a bag around to some nutter?'

'Like Keith says, this fella asked me to take a hold-all to another fella's house. It made me curious – the weight. I went into a lane, unzipped it. There was nothin' but bullets and a hand-gun. Maybe I shoulda dumped the load. But I was rightly landed. When I got to where I was goin' the fella asked me in for a cuppa and a wee chat about football. We went into the kitchen. He said nothin' about the hold-all. Just put it in a cupboard. The back door was open . . .'

13

'You should have run for it,' interrupted Gavin.'

'I didn't know what to say . . . "Aye, lovely flowers you got there," I stuttered.

' "Yeah, they're not bad."

' "They look dynamite," I blurted.

' "Yeah, that's what's buried underneath them."

'I wasn't long about gettin' outa the place. . . Lesson is, you shouldn't let homesickness get to you. Maybe you wouldn't have the same kinda trouble I had in Belfast. But trouble's everywhere. It's always just around the corner, especially for the likes of us. You should appreciate comin' to a place like this: nice digs, nice club, prospects of a decent future. Got the drift?'

Hammer had most certainly got the drift.

Tea finished, they went upstairs to get ready to go out and celebrate Gavin's elevation to the profesional football ranks. For a few hours, at least, Hammer forgot all about home and Sandy Black's unfortunate encounter with the unsavoury elements that lurked in Northern Ireland.

London Albion's training ground at Highfield was chock-a-block with photographers and a training crew. All the interest was in the first-team squad. There was a photo-call and an interview with team manager John Warner and some of the club's top players. The second team and Youth side were virtually ignored.

The new season was about to start in a week's time. Pre-season training was finished. The first team had been away and played in a tournament in Tokyo against top Italian and Dutch opposition. The reserves had had a few friendly games against non-league opposition, while the Youths were confined to the training ground. Physically they had trained very hard. Extra coaches were brought in and a lot of emphasis was put on technical skills. There had been a ball to every player, with the goalkeepers being worked on separately. They had two hours in the morning with a short break. Then in the afternoon there was always a punishing physical session – lapping the training grounds, trotting, sprinting, trotting, sprinting, with the squad broken up into sparse relay teams, racing one against the other, and individually against the trainer's stop-watch.

The photo-call was almost over. The first-team squad had finished theirs. Then it was the turn of the second team. The first-team captain and some of the top players were still being interviewed and posing for the cameras.

Eventually the Youth team had their photo-call. There was an interview with a local radio station. How did they think they would fare for the season? 'Great,' said Stevie Hodgson, the Youth-team manager. 'We've got one of our strongest Youth squads for seasons.'

'Is there any truth in the rumour that a few of your Youth team are on the verge of breaking through on to the first-team squad?'

'No, no truth whatsoever.'

'Is it true the FA are particularly keen you don't play your English-born Youth players at a higher level this season?'

'Not true. Anyway, we wouldn't allow the FA to dictate to us.'

'We hear there are a few outstanding players on your Youth side. Who are they?'

'They are all outstanding. We regard the whole squad as outstanding. Like I said, the squad's the strongest we've had in years.'

'You hope to win the FA Youth Cup?'

'No, we expect to win it.'

'The grapevine has it that you have an outstanding prospect in the squad. Which one is he?'

'Like I said, the whole squad's outstanding.'

'This kid's Irish. How many Irish kids are in the squad?'

'Just three.'

'Which of the three is he?'

'No comment.'

'Can we interview them?'

'No, Youth-team players are not allowed to be interviewed . . . except with my permission.'

'Can we have permission, then?'

'No.'

'When's your season start?'

'Early next week. First match against Chelsea Youths, Stamford Bridge, Tuesday night, KO seven-fifteen. Report on the match.'

'Can we interview the kids after it?'

'Definitely not.'

The radio interview finished. The Youths jogged off in their green and white tracksuits. The radio crew scowled after them, wondering which of the eighteen was the Irish kid – the new sensation they had heard about.

Next day, Gavin and Hammer flew out from Heathrow with the full Youth squad to take part in a tournament in Holland. They won, and the team coach regarded it as a good omen for the rest of the season.

Stevie Hodgson, Bill Thornbull and the rest of the backroom staff were well pleased. They had two objectives in mind; to win the FA Youth Cup, and to see that the team's two best prospects, Gavin and anchor-man Mick Bates, weren't exposed to the media. Stevie Hodgson was to act as an overseer, to see that they came through the season fresh and strong, without any undue media attention which would affect their form. Gavin was to be eased along gradually, so that he would be able to withstand the growing publicity sure to surround him the following season when it was planned to bring him closer to first-team status.

Gavin knew very little of this plan, which was the way the club wanted it. He was better not knowing, not until it was about to happen, and then, hopefully, he would be mature enough to handle the whole hocus-pocus. Publicity was great, but it could ruin a young unprotected footballer.

Under the terms of his professional contract, Gavin had received a big jump in wages. He could have considered a flat, or even buying a house. But instead he stayed in digs with Hammer, Keith and Sandy. The club wouldn't have it any other way. They felt that Gavin was too young to be allowed go out on his own. He would be kept in check under the watchful eye of Mrs Burtinshaw. The club expected a nice return on his future, and were not going to have some overcurious newsmen, or money, ruin him. Footballers there were plenty, but very few as promising, or as talented, as Gavin.

In the meantime, Gavin could hardly wait for the match against Chelsea Youths to come around. He was straining on the leash, hungry for the season to start.

2

Elaine Clarke, a rising star in the athletics world – a notable performer at both athletics and soccer – jogged along Blacklion, past the picture-house, in the direction of the railway bridge and the turn-off which led on to the path for the Cliff Walk. She sometimes trained on the Cliff Walk and over the tough mountain terrain of Bray Head. She regulated her breathing as she ran: long, sharp, relaxed draughts of air, occasionally holding a breath a few seconds longer than the norm. Tuesday she was doing some stamina training, the sloping run up the side of Bray Head was good for that. Normally she was into speed training: 200-400 metre lapped runs, flat out. Usually when she speed-trained her father accompanied her, stop-watch in hand, urging her to run faster, regulate her breathing more evenly, improve her running rhythm. In training, 400 metre lap-circuits flat out were tough – the toughest of the lot, especially when she had to run three or four after very short intervals.

She had just come to the end of her summer athletics season, running 800 metre races for Crusaders in Dublin. She had done well. She had run at Youth and Junior level, with a few Senior races thrown in. Not bad for a kid who had just turned seventeen. But she wasn't entirely satisfied. She thought she could do a lot better. She felt that, maybe, she should move up to 1500 metres. She consulted her club coach.

'You're young. Wait.'

'I'm missing that extra turn of pace for 800 metres. I think I should move up.'

'You're too young for longer distance races. You haven't

got the strength yet. You're competing against girls older than you most of the time. Anyway, you're playing too much soccer. I told you to quit soccer. Were you playing last Sunday?'

Elaine didn't answer that one. Of course she had been playing soccer last Sunday. A friendly for Brighton Celtic against a team from Booterstown. She had scored two goals. Brighton Celtic were due to play a Ladies Football Association of Ireland Cup game against a Premier side, Wellsox from Limerick, in a few weeks time. She didn't tell her coach about that one. But she would have to make a decision between soccer and athletics soon. She was due to sit her Leaving Cert in June – maybe after that, or maybe after next summer's athletic season. Maybe after winter training and a switch up to 1500 metres to see how her finishing kick would compare with the competition. Or should she leave it until early December next year, just after the outdoor track season would come to an end.

She had already put the decision off several times and her athletics coach was rapidly losing patience with her. Brighton Celtic and some of the officials of the LFAI were pressurizing her too. They wanted her to concentrate on soccer. They felt she was on the verge of making the Irish Ladies soccer team. Either way, she determined, the decision would be hers, not one fashioned by her parents, her athletics coach, or the Ladies soccer authorities. Though she did feel concern for her father. She could only hope he wouldn't be upset with her final choice of sports. An ex-professional who had been on the coaching staff of Coventry City, where Elaine had been brought up, he had always taken a keen interest in her sporting career. She had played soccer since she was seven, and had joined Coventry Godiva athletics club at ten years of age. Her family had moved back to Ireland when she was fourteen. She missed England, but only in a sporting sense. Sports were much better organized there and the competition was

19

tougher. Ireland was much more easy-going, more relaxing. And the pressures weren't the same. But she wasn't complaining.

Normally on a Saturday afternoon during school term Elaine would be in Bray playing hockey for her school, Loreto. But in early September the school term had just begun and the hockey season wouldn't start for another few weeks. So she decided to go for a run out along the Cliff Walk and the Greystones side of Bray Head. She looked really hip in her training-gear: A Frank Shorter Logo T-shirt and a blue pair of Roadsters. She was in top condition after a reasonably successful athletics season.

A short way out, where a headland jutted out from the Cliff Walk, she came across Luke. His bike, which was propped up against a thicket of ferns, had an aluminium pigeon-basket on the back-carrier. He was probably scouting for stray pigeons from a pigeon-race earlier in the day. The young bird races always came to a conclusion in early September, and a lot of birds hadn't the strength, or the guile, to make it back to the home lofts. It was a sad reflection on the hobby that so many young birds were entered for races they hadn't an earthly of finishing.

Luke looked slightly uneasy when he saw Elaine. Not that she was put out. Luke always looked uneasy. He wasn't about to change overnight. Elaine was well used to his shyness. It didn't matter a toss to her.

'Out looking for pigeons?'

'Yeah.'

'Haven't you enough of them already?'

'Sure I have. I might give a few to kids. I don't like to see them suffer, that's all. Some of them that'd come down here'd never make it home. Some might survive in the wild, but not them all . . . I heard from Hammer yesterday.'

'How's he getting on?'

'Settlin' in. Bit early yet, but he thinks he'll stick it out.'

'That's good,' beamed Elaine. 'He likes it, then?'

'Yeah. He thinks it's great. He asked for you.'

'That's nice. I hear Lar Holmes is starting up a team again.'

'Him!'

Luke didn't get on with Lar Holmes. It was why Luke had lost interest in football and didn't play any more. He had taken up pigeon-racing instead.

'He did a lot for all of you a few years ago.'

'Not for me.'

'There's no need to talk like that. I'm thinking of giving him a hand training the team. I know if Gavin and Hammer were here they'd give him a hand. Jake would too.'

'Jake shouldn't be let near football. He'd get the whole club banned. Anyway, haven't you enough on your plate without gettin' involved runnin' a football team with Lar Holmes?'

'I'm a bit muddled over athletics at the moment. I don't know what I want. I feel I might do better if I were to move from 800 to 1500 metres. I think I'd have the staying power for 1500 metres. I'm beginning to feel 800 metres is not my true distance. Anyway, I'm getting too much pressure from my coach lately. Giving Lar Holmes a hand with his football team might help relax me – take the strain off the athletics side of things.'

'There's more to life than athletics, Elaine.'

'So there is . . . Going to Scorpion Jack's gig in Bray tonight?'

'What gig?'

'Saturday night – Bray. Didn't Jake tell you about the Green Door?'

'No. I haven't seen much of him lately. He's too tied up with his band.'

Elaine only half believed him. It seemed to her that he was the one who was tied up, totally obsessed with his pigeons or, in any spare moment he might have, brooding over some imaginary misfortune.

'I'm going to the gig. You can come into Bray with me.'

'You'll be with your friends.'

'They won't bite you. Anyway, if you're there, my father is picking me up afterwards. You can have a lift home. Or, maybe, you'd rather go home with Jake?'

'Again he gets the gear packed into the van and finished talkin' and that . . . I'd be there until three in the mornin'. I'd be murdered goin' home that late.'

'Good, you can come home with my Da.'

'I don't know, Elaine. But thanks anyway.'

'Don't mention it. You could do with getting away from those pigeons. They'll drive you looney yet. See you in Bray tonight.'

'Maybe.'

Elaine left Luke where he was. Something of a hermit in the wilderness. She veered off the Cliff Walk up on to the gruelling slopes of Bray Head.

Luke watched her go. He wished he wasn't so damned unsociable. Although he wouldn't admit to it, the only time he felt at ease was when he was around pigeons. Elaine was a nice kid. She probably had quite a few admirers in Bray. Those Bray lads gave him the shudders. To hell with them anyway. He was just as good as any of them. Maybe he'd go to the dance. Damned sure he'd go. He was no John Travolta. But he was just as entitled to some Saturday-night fever as the next fellow. He'd go. Anyway Jake would be glad to see him there.

Maybe the dance would do something for his inhibitions.

The Green Door Rock Club was at the Albert Walk in Bray, just a few yards from the Dart station. The premises was small enough. There were the customary fire exits, a mineral bar, a fair-sized dance floor with intermixing lights which made the place surreal. The stage had just about enough room to set up the band equipment, less than enough room for a rock band to get hyped up.

Scorpion Jack consisted of four band members: Liam on drums, Kev on rhythm guitar, Dave on bass guitar, Jake on lead guitar. Dave and Jake alternated the lead-singer role. Kev could sing too, but he kept mainly to backing, a task Dave and Jake took turns sharing when not on lead. The band was managed by Kev's father but only on a temporary basis until, hopefully, some top-grade management team would replace him. Kev's father was an ex-musician himself, having played on the beat-club and showband scene in the early sixties. In fact he had played at the Green Door as a teenager when it had gone under another guise. And that was Scorpion Jack, apart from the fact that they played a lot of their own compositions, Jake composing the music while Dave worked on the lyrics.

Scorpion Jack always travelled to their gigs in a fruit and vegetable van belonging to a friend of one of Dave's brothers. They felt a bit embarrassed about the van, especially as it had a banana and apple logo on the side, and usually tried to get their gear into a gig well before any fans would come on the scene. They were acutely aware that the van decoration could affect their image, and inspire malicious remarks from rival bands.

'They might start callin' us the "Fruit an' Nutters",' grimaced Jake. 'Keep that van outa sight, especially when we're playin' around Dublin. I wouldn't give the bastards the pleasure.'

Scorpion Jack had their amplifiers, mikes and instruments in place by eight-thirty. A few quick chords of music to make sure the amplifiers were functioning properly, then they struck into a Rolling Stones number, 'Little Red Rooster'. Jake took the vocals. Somebody's guitar was out of tune – Kev's. 'Little Red Rooster' stopped in midflow.

'Get the chord right on that guitar. What are you tryin' to do, drive the punters away? It sounds like a cat with its tail stuck in a mangler. Tune the damned chord.'

'No bother. Some kid's been messin' with it. Put it down, someone picks it up an' starts messin'. Knocks the whole thing off-key.'

'Nobody's been here to mess.'

'No, they're all outside waitin' to come in.'

The gig was due to start at nine. Already there was a crowd outside. Admittedly not huge, but they were all Scorpion Jack fans. Kids from sixteen to eighteen, mainly pals, associates, friends of friends. The Green Door was strictly membership, strictly non-alcoholic. So those kids who took a drink shared a can while they waited for the doors of the club to open. No way was anyone going to smuggle cans inside and hide them in the toilets. They were all afraid of the club's bouncer, 'Big Red' and his reputation as a hard-hitting boozer. He had a great nose for drink. He could sniff it out anywhere. So the kids just weren't into smuggling alcohol into the Green Door. They just hadn't the generosity of heart to give 'Big Red' a free night of alcoholic bliss. Apart from alcohol he had a punch like a sledge-hammer, and one other major characteristic – a gigantic red nose; thus his nickname.

The gig was to run from nine to eleven-thirty. This particular Saturday night was very special for Scorpion Jack. The main band had pulled out at short notice and Scorpion Jack were asked to fill the gig on their own. They were topping the bill, so to speak, no mean feat for a new group.

'Sure you can do it,' asked the club manager.

'Of course. We can walk on water, ye know.'

'Yeah, walk on it. Run on it. And drown in it.'

Kev, by now, had sorted out the rebel guitar-chord.

'What happened to "Little Red Rooster"?'

'Liam wrung its neck.'

Instead they moved into 'Roll over Beethoven'.

'What's this? A Golden Oldies bash?'

'No, the resurrection of John Lennon.'

Scorpion Jack didn't normally play rock classics, but when they played at the Green Door they liked to throw in a few for sentimental reasons, mainly for Kev's father. Anyway, they liked old rock numbers. Their own compositions apart, they were the best.

'Turn down the volume on that amp,' shouted Dave to Jake. 'It's far too loud. The sound of it'd turn Michael Jackson Chinese.'

'Want a takeaway then?'

'Turn it down.'

Fifteen minutes later, Scorpion Jack had all the hitches ironed out. They were ready to perform. It was time to open the doors.

Fifteen minutes later the Green Door was jammed tight.

Elaine was there. Luke too. Elaine was with some friends from Bray. Luke hadn't a clue who they were. But he sat with them for a while. All went well until a few college hunks came over and began to chat-up Elaine and her friends. Luke felt it was time to move off.

The music was beginning to liven up. A few head-shakers were out on the floor stomping and letting themselves go wild. Apart from the Bray and Greystones contingents the rest of the kids were from Shankill. They had come into Bray on the Dart – and had a habit of travelling free of charge. It was very easy to 'negotiate' Shankill station, if not the ticket-collector in Bray. But when there was a crowd going through the gate at Bray it was more or less impossible for the ticket-collector to cope.

'Always travel in numbers. It's cheaper that way.'

Luke went and stood near the corner of the stage. He recognized a fellow who used to catch pigeons down at Bray harbour. They got talking. They hadn't much to say – just a general drift of conversation. Most of it was muffled by the number Scorpion Jack was playing. Either way the conversation wouldn't have lasted. 'Big Red' came across and told them not to be blocking the side of the stage. Luke went back to the mineral bar. Elaine was out on the floor dancing with one of the college hunks. He got a coke and sat at a separate table. Two girl punks came into the club and sat beside him at the table. They were two rough-looking gals. They had had trouble getting into the gig. The doorman didn't fancy letting them in. They had no membership cards and, on appearance, he classified them as undesirables. They had to bribe a few lads who were going into the gig to vouch that they were their sisters.

'They're two nurses. It's their night off.'

The two spiky-haired girls passed the doorman, 'Big Red' also, and walked into the dance area. They drew a few stares, but they didn't mind in the least. They were what a connoisseur would term 'Liberated Women'; by the look of them, they were just after liberating the French Foreign Legion. They sat beside Luke.

They were big fans of Jake and Scorpion Jack. They had first heard the band at a gig in Dublin, made inquiries, and decided to come out to Scorpion Jack's heartland in Bray. Six of their friends had intended to come out from Dublin too, but the busman wouldn't let them on the bus. So the two girls travelled on their own. They absolutely raved over Jake.

'Isn't he gorgeous. Jus' look at tha' lovely black hair. He's real romantic lookin'. Jus' like yer man outa wha'yecall it, Wutherin' Heights. Wha's his name? Hotcliff, or somethin'?'

'Heathcliff.'

'He ain't half a smasher.'

'Lovely.'

'Gorgeous.'

'He used to play football, ye know. Gave it up 'cause it got in the way of his music. Gave it all up for the sake of rock 'n' roll.'

'Maria, I love the way ye said tha': "Gave it all up for rock 'n' roll." You make it sound as if he's Jimi Hendrix.'

'He is. He's a dream.'

Luke was in half a mind to run for it. Maybe the crowd, and Elaine in particular, would think that the two punks were with him. Worse, she might think he was going with one of them. People were looking. Even Elaine, in a kind of way.

Scorpion Jack were into a fast set. Liam was going mental on drums; Kev straight-faced, his fingers tight to the fret, holding a note that extra second longer. Dave was cool. Jake in a frenzy. The amplifiers blasted, the rhythm of the music came over sharp and strong.

'Let it rip, man.'

Straight away there was catastrophe. One of the punks asked Luke for a dance. He wasn't in a position to refuse.

Worse, when they were out on the floor the other punk got lonesome and joined in.

The floor cleared. All that was left was Luke and the two punks.

Jake kept the set going on purpose. It seemed to go on and on. Bon Jovi, Deacon Blue, Dire Straits, they were all belted out. Jake thought it a great laugh.

But little did he realize the laugh was to be on him.

The two punks, Maria and her friend, in the dying seconds of a Scorpion Jack original, abandoned Luke and made a dash for the stage and the comfort of Jake's arms.

There was bedlam.

Jake nearly had a seizure.

'Big Red' came hurtling across the dance floor. Jake's guitar would have been smashed to bits if Dave hadn't grabbed it before the two punks got to wrap themselves around Jake.

'Oh, Jake, the music is smashin'! Yer hair is smashin'! Everythin's smashin'. We love you!'

'Big Red' wasn't feeling quite so amorous though. He

grabbed Maria in an armlock. The other punk bit him on the hand and he let go. Maria then turned around and kneed him in the groin. His face contorted with pain and he fell straight off the stage.

Luke felt as embarrassed as hell. He edged away from the action. Next thing he felt a tap on his shoulder.

'You're with them.'

'With who?'

'With the two punks.'

'No, I'm not!'

'You are! And you're barred!'

Luke was escorted to the door and put outside.

Meanwhile back on stage Maria and her friend were lording it. They were all smiles and coos at Jake and company.

Meanwhile, 'Big Red' had got his second wind. He attempted a lunge at Maria. This time he had plenty of support from Kev's father and the fellow who was serving behind the mineral bar. The two girls were quickly subdued and escorted outside. Luke kept his distance from them. The club management were in tow. They asked the two punks if they were going to behave. If not, the police would be called. The girls decided to go peacefully. They gave 'Big Red' a look of defiance and went up the Albert Walk to the railway station to get the Dart back into Dublin.

'Know wha', Maria?'

'Wha'?'

'Sometimes I wish I was born a fella. An' know wha' I do?'

'No, wha'?'

'I'd clobber tha' bouncer righ' on his big red snout. The size of it! It'd do justice to one of them Cruise missiles the Americans used to drop on Baghdad.'

Apart from Maria and her friend the gig wasn't quite over. The time was only nine-forty. The dance settled back to normality Jake, Dave, Kev and Liam got back into the groove. They had been slightly taken aback by the charge of the two punks on to the stage. But not as much as Kev's father. He didn't want any recurrence in the future. He only hoped Scorpion Jack weren't attracting the wrong kind of clientele.

Poor Luke was forgotten about outside the club door. That is, except by Elaine. She went outside and was shocked to find that he was barred. She went to see Jake. Jake immediately took the matter up with 'Big Red' and the club manager. Explained that it was all a mistake, that Luke had nothing to do with the punks; that he was a personal friend of the band. Luke was allowed back inside. Elaine kept him company, more to cheer him up than anything else.

When the gig was over he got a lift back to Greystones with Elaine and her father. He was damned if he was going to wait around all night for Jake to load the gear into the fruit and vegetable van, give Liam a lift home to Shankill, and all the rest of it. In fact, he was damned if he was ever going to go to the Green Door again. And sure as hell he wasn't going to get into any more trouble. He'd keep to his pigeons. His mind was in a total state of turmoil.

He slept it out until late on Sunday morning.

Elaine went down to the Railway Field to give Lar Holmes a hand with his new U-12 football team.

London Albion's Youths were given preferential treatment for the opening league fixture against Chelsea Youths at Stamford Bridge. They travelled in the luxury of the coach usually reserved for the first team. The decor was plush, with Pullman seats, CD and video facilities. There was even a toilet and a small bar. Of course, the bar was out of bounds to the Youths. But it was nice to travel on the same coach London Albion's much vaunted first-team squad used week in, week out. Most of the squad were internationals, household names of British soccer.

The Youths didn't expect many spectators to be at the game. maybe a hundred or so. But rumour had it that the London Albion board of directors would be there to wish the team luck. Something like when a ship was launched and sent sliding into the sea on its first voyage. It would be something similar with the directors. Some shaking of hands, a few words of encouragement. Duty done they would possibly struggle through the effort of watching the game and disappear into the directors' lounge afterwards. They would hardly know any of the players by name, except to say that the centre-forward was good, or lousy, or whatever. Maybe they would take note of a name and over the course of the season enquire how that particular player was progressing. But usually they weren't into names, unless the name was a big card draw that they could invite to some party so as to impress the guests and add to their own personal ego. The blunt truth, from a director's perspective, was that Youth team names were not really worth remembering. There were plenty of fish in the sea, so to speak; mostly of the same ilk; and most would fail to make the grade at top level. Professional football was regarded as a glamour sport. But then, glamour always had to be fought for and won. And even at that it wouldn't last for ever. It was tough to get to the top, tough to stay there, but the climbdown was even tougher. Tough life. Tough luck.

But the only thing London Albion Youths had on their minds was the seven-fifteen kick-off. London Albion v Chelsea; the Albinos v the Pensioners. First match of the season, a London derby game. All London games were always something to relish, especially the Spurs and Arsenal fixtures. The luxury coach snaked through the London tea-time traffic, with eighteen players on board.

30

Eighteen young hopefuls! Stevie Hodgson and Bill Thornbull sat up front.

Stevie and Bill weren't the only mentors travelling. Two of the coaching staff were also present. They both had notepads cushioned in the inside pockets of their neat London Albion club blazers. Stevie Hodgson wasn't averse to carrying a notebook either. They weren't just for fun. They were used to jot down details of each player's performance – this was standard practice for all matches during the season. Back at Highfield the notes would be translated into graph form, showing the performance level for each player, every week over the course of the season. Talk about being put under the microscope! The pressure was always on the Youths to play well.

The first time Hammer saw Stevie and company tricking with performance graphs the sight made him tense up.

'Relax. Don't worry,' advised Gavin.

'Just think, you're out there playin' and they're assessin' you all the time. They're only puttin' you off your game.'

'You'll just have to learn to put up with it.'

'Sure, either that or turn into a nervous wreck with worry. What are they tryin' to do, put us off football altogether?'

'Just part of the scene. Forget about it.'

Wisely, Hammer tried to put the idea of notes, graphs and records of players' individual performances to the back of his mind. Most of the others players, including Gavin, were well used to being scrutinized by Stevie Hodgson and the coaching staff. But not Hammer. He was new to the scene.

The team had something of a joker among the pack. Well, something of a prankster. Glenn Thomas was his name. He was down to play beside Hammer at the centre of the defence. He was a current Welsh Youth inter-national and very strong both on the ground and in the air. He was always a good laugh, though he never allowed a situation to deteriorate into a shambles. Stevie Hodgson tolerated Glenn because his humour was good for the team. It balanced the serious side of running a team – especially a Youth side who were in the throes of attempting to make it in the ruthless world of professional football. Yes, the right blend of humour, properly delivered, was always a tonic through the stress every professional footballer had to endure, through the bleakness of a loss of form, injury, or being dropped from the team.

On the coach on the way to Stamford Bridge Glenn had spotted a man in overalls carrying an eight-foot plank along the footpath.

'Look, he's goin' to a board-meeting.'

'Probably Chelsea's.'

'Yeah, the plank's about that thick all right.'

It wasn't usual for Welshmen to have a sense of humour. But Glenn was an exception – a howl.

'Hey, Gavin. You like Chelsea.'

'Not really.'

'I'd say Sandy does.'

'I don't.'

'Strange. Chelsea's Shed gang have all got degrees in Irish politics. They once had an Irish full-back.'

'Paddy Mulligan, wasn't it?'

'No, Paddy the Irishman.'

When they got to Stamford Bridge they weren't long in togging out. They hadn't too much time before kick-off. Only twenty minutes. Stevie gave a pep-talk: 'Get stuck in. Move the ball wide. Use the flanks. Glenn, talk Hammer through the game.'

'I don't need to be talked through the game.'

'No?'

'I'll be all right.'

'Just give him some encouragement, Glenn.'

'I'll give him my last Rolo.'

The stench of wintergreen was beginning to fill the dressing-room. Some of the players were dowsing themselves in the stuff, almost as lavishly as a male model used after-shave.

'John and Keith, not too much of the overlap. They're quick on the break. Spray the ball about as much as possible. Don't let the game get cluttered. Gavin, be on your toes. And Cyril, concentrate – try and read the situation in advance.'

'Yes, Boss,' they answered back in unison.

The gear was kind of glossy – a brand new strip. Green and white striped shirts, green knicks and white socks. Bill Thornbull had laid it all out on the dressing-room bench with the jersey numbers showing on top. All they had to do was pick it up and put it on.

'New gear. Mine's perfumed.'

'Look, mine's got a price-tag on the collar.'

'How much?'

'I'm only jokin'.'

'Stevie, I need a pair of new boots. Any chance of the club buyin' me a pair of new boots?'

'Not likely.'

Now they had their shin-guards in place, tie-ups seen to. Then deep into some warm-up and stretch exercises.

Poor Sandy Black sat in the corner with the remaining three players who had failed to make the subs' bench. He hadn't made the team. He hadn't even made the subs. He was relegated to spectator status, doomed to watch the match from the stand. He felt very disappointed, because away from home most teams played an extra defender, or at worse kept a spare defender on the subs' bench. It was a bitter pill to swallow. But he was prepared to persevere. Sandy was made of stern stuff – he wasn't a quitter.

The buzzer went in the dressing-room. It was time to get out on the pitch. But not before the referee came in and inspected their studs, etcetera. The directors had arrived too. A few quick handshakes, words of encouragement, then off to the directors' box. Maybe they'd be back again at full-time, and that would be it for the season, unless they got to the semi-final, or final, of the FA Youth Cup. Stevie Hodgson would need security guards on the dressing-room doors to keep the directors out if that scenario ever arose.

The players trooped out in single file into the corridor. They waited for Stevie, Bill Thornbull and the two coaches to come after them. Then they turned directly into the corridor which led out on to the pitch. As they had anticipated, there weren't many spectators. Apart from the directors and a few club officials Chelsea's three-tier main stand was empty. The stand opposite was just as bad. There were a few in the Shed-end though. Nothing that anyone short on concentration would have trouble in counting.

Chelsea were already out on the pitch, warming up and having a kick-about. Their team seemed to be much the same as in the previous season, though they had a few new faces.

'Look! Chelsea's baby-snatchin',' pointed Mick Bates. 'Tha' titch over there looks only fourteen. They musta snatched 'im from outside a Marks and Spencers. 'is Mum'll come lookin' for 'im afore 'alf-time.'

Some of the players looked. Mick was correct. No way did the 'titch' look Youth-team material. He looked more like an U-14, even an U-12. Chelsea must have been hard up, they felt. Kids like that just weren't produced on Youth teams. Chelsea should have sent him back to his schoolboy team.

'Maybe he's a dwarf,' joked Glenn Thomas.

'Aw, shut up.'

The match went well for London Albion. Being start of season everyone was fresh and keen – even the Chelsea playboys. The score was 1-1 at half-time. Cyril Stevens scored off a miskick by the Chelsea goalkeeper, who had attempted to clear the ball in a hurry from a back pass. The clearance fell straight to Cyril Stevens. And from all of twenty yards he returned the ball past the bewildered goalkeeper, straight into the net. The kid Mick Bates had pointed out in the kick-about equalized for Chelsea on the stroke of half-time. He weaved through the London Albion defence, Hammer included, and cheekily side-stepped the ball into the net.

Stevie Hodgson was reasonably pleased with the team's first-half performance. Apart from the wonder-kid's goal Hammer had shown up pretty well. The new goalkeeper, Jeff Harker, had played very soundly. Mick Bates, as usual, had thrived in midfield. And Gavin, up front, showed a nice understanding with Cyril Stevens.

London Albion played even better in the second half. Stevie Hodgson made a quick substitution. He took off one of the younger midfield players and moved a sub into the left-full position, pushing Keith Jardine forward to put the shackles on the Chelsea wonder-kid, who was having things pretty much his own way. The ploy worked. Chelsea lost their momentum and London Albion dominated the remainder of the game. Gavin rammed in a goal: 1-2. John Palmer got a third, straight off an intended cross. Mick Bates wrapped it up with goal number four. But Chelsea came back and scored a second goal off an indirect free. The game finished 2-4.

It was a good team performance. A good competitive debut by the new boys, Hammer and Jeff Harker. Stevie Hodgson and Bill Thornbull were well pleased. Pre-season indications had been confirmed. London Albion's Youths were on the verge of being something special.

The season continued. The Youth team played three more matches – won one, drew one, and lost one: Portsmouth, Wimbledon and West Ham, in that order.

Then they played Fulham. Gavin scored a cracker of a goal on the volley from twenty-five yards. London Albion won 1-0. But after the Fulham match the cat was out of the bag; Keith Jardine intended signing professional forms for Glasgow Rangers. He didn't tell Stevie Hodgson or the coaching staff. He just mentioned it on the quiet to Gavin, Hammer and Sandy. Told them to say nothing.

'You'll have to tell Stevie and John Warner.'

'Naw. I'll just leave. I'm goin' back to Scotland to-morrow.'

'You'd better see Stevie first.'

'Och, I don't wanna see anyone. I'll just go home.'

'You'll have to go to John Warner's office and tell him.'

Next day, Keith went to John Warner's office. There was an uproar. A phone-call to Keith's parents, followed by a phone-call to Glasgow Rangers. There was blue murder on the phone.

'He isn't leaving Brompton.'

'He wants to.'

'He isn't leaving and that's final.'

'He wants to come to us.'

'I'll have you reported to UEFA.'

'Do what you like. It's his choice.'

'Do you want to go, Keith?'

'Aya, I wanna . . .Sorry . . . Can I go now?'

'To where?'

'Back to the digs.'

'Keith, think about it. You'd be foolish to leave. Football opportunities are better this side of the Border.'

'I wanna go back to Scotland.'

'Think it over. Let me know Saturday. Kids . . .! Not one of you seem to know what you want.'

Keith left the office. He went back to Scotland that Saturday. Gavin, Hammer and Sandy went to Euston with him for the Glasgow train. They wished him well and said good-bye.

Life went on without Keith. But his departure had one good consequence. John Palmer moved over to left-full leaving the right-full position vacant for Sandy Black. Sandy's confidence grew and within weeks he was playing better than ever. He was back in the team on a regular basis.

Keith wrote for a while. but after that all correspondence ceased. They never heard much of him after that. Some say he ended up in the Scottish Second Division playing for Cowdenbeath. One thing, he never played for Scotland except for a handful of matches at Youth level.

Football-wise everything began to go well for London Albion's Youths. The routine for the season was established, except that in the evenings most of the squad, Gavin, Hammer and Sandy included, had to study for their GCSEs.

But Gavin, at least, wasn't complaining. He was a full-time professional with a contract and a good wage. He wasn't an apprentice any more, tied to the club on a Youth Training scheme.

The others had the example of Gavin and Mike Bates to inspire them. There could be heartbreak, but there was also light at the end of the tunnel. In the meantime, the incentive was there to train hard and hope to be one of the lucky ones who would make it to the top. There wouldn't be many who would make it all the way. But, at least, they could try.

3

Elaine decided to put athletics on the back-burner, at least until the Leaving Cert was over at the end of June. Instead she intended to play the occasional game for Brighton Celtic and give Lar Holmes a hand to train Shamrock Boys U-12s. In the end her mind was largely made up for her because of a row she had with her athletics coach. Her coach wanted her to go into Dublin two nights a week for specialized training. Elaine felt that to be a bit too much, especially as she was studying for her exam. The extra training just wasn't on.

'I wouldn't have the time.'

'Make the time.'

'To hell I will.'

'You'll be almost guaranteed a scholarship to Villanova if you come through with the required times.'

'It could mean I'd fail my Leaving.'

'Maybe Saturday and Sunday instead?'

Elaine was slow to answer.

'Sunday is football, isn't it?'

Yes, Sunday was football and Elaine's team, Brighton Celtic, had just beaten Wellsox in the LFAI Cup. They were through to the quarter-final.

'I told you to give up football. You can't mix both sports. Not at this point in time. It'll have to be either football or athletics. This special training is to run until the beginning of the summer athletics season. You'll have to have your times down by the summer.'

'I was thinking of moving up to 1500 metres.'

'Suit yourself. But you'll have to make a choice. You'll have to do as I say or forget about it.'

Elaine consulted her Mum and Dad, half afraid they'd put undue pressure on her by asking her to go for the week-end coaching sessions. But they told her to make her own decision. Do whatever she thought best. She was lucky to have such understanding parents. She knew of a few kids good at sport whose parents pressurized them solely to satisfy their own personal egos. Luckily hers weren't that way inclined. The decision would be hers, and hers alone.

Elaine chose soccer. Well, that was the way she put it. The Leaving Cert was more to the forefront of her mind. What she really intended was to put her studies first. Sit the Leaving Cert in June and, maybe, get back into athletics after that. But the incident left a sour taste. She didn't feel too happy about her coach. If she got back into the swing of things after her exam she definitely wouldn't train under the same coach. She would join a different club instead. Who wanted to be dictated to and put under too much pressure? Life was tough enough without that kind of hassle.

Elaine's first serious session giving Lar Holmes a hand with his new U-12 squad was on a Sunday morning a few weeks after Scorpion Jack's gig at the Green Door. The squad was very much a mixed bag – largely indifferent, unbalanced and of a poor playing standard. But as the season wasn't due to start for another few weeks that gave Lar and Elaine some breathing space to get the team into shape.

Jake had promised Elaine he'd be on the lookout for new players. He was good at unearthing talent as all the kids in Greystones were mad about him. He was a Pied Piper type of character. The team wasn't completely useless though, Gavin's brother, Gary, being one of the few players who was up to the required standard. Gary was a good player, a centre-forward, but not of the calibre to play at the very top schoolboy level like Gavin had done.

Straight away Elaine could see there were problems. Not only with the team, but also with Lar Holmes' abrupt manner. Old habits die hard. Elaine would have to work hard on both the team and Lar Holmes' infamous habit of shouting at kids.

'We'll keep the two fulls. They can be worked on,' observed Elaine. 'At least four other players are needed. A centre-half who can dominate the defence. Someone up front with pace to play off Gavin's brother.The midfield's not the best either. It needs a ball-winner and someone to give it some shape. Have you got plenty of registration forms?'

'Wait until we find out what league we're in first. I'll sign them all together.'

'You haven't signed any players yet?'

'No. Not until I find out if we're in Dublin or Wicklow. I can't see any other club bein' in a hurry to sign our lot. We'll know which league we're in in a few days. We'll sign up the players then.'

Elaine got the session going in earnest. She demonstrated how to shield the ball and lay it off and run into space for a return pass. She looked complete class in her Sky Blues tracksuit, much too pacy and skilled for the kids she was trying to instruct. Most of them hadn't got the basic skills such as ball control and passing ability. As for their positioning, the defence was a shambles. They were all over the place; they were all ball-watchers, and worse, ball-chasers. Judging by the standard of play on view it was extremely unlikely that they would ever make a team.

Twenty minutes later two new kids arrived.

'Where do you play?'

'We both play midfield. We like to set things up and get stuck in. We don't like refs that keep blowin' up. We like to get on with the match. We've no time for fancy stuff either. We like to keep the game movin' and wallop the other team.'

'How come you've never been down here before?'

'We just moved out from Dublin. This fellow said he'd give us twenty fags if we came down here and signed on.'

'What's his name?'

'Jake Flynn, he said.'

Five minutes later another kid arrived. He was wearing a tracksuit with his football gear underneath. He was sucking a lollipop. In fact, he had a bag full of lollipops.

'What age are you?'

'Nine.'

'Who sent you?'

'Some man called Jake.'

'Did he give you the lollipops?'

'Yeah. He said he'd give me six more if I made the team.'

'Ever play on a team before?'

'Not really, my Mammy wouldn't let me.'

'How come she changed her mind?'

'Mr Jake said the man that runs the team used to play for Manchester United.'

Elaine looked at Lar Holmes. They laughed. Another of Jake's infamous lies.

'What position do you think you should play?'

'Forward.'

'You're giving away three years. We'll try you out on the wing. What foot do you kick with?'

'Both. But I score better goals with my right. I use my right from far out. I only use my left close in.'

Far out! thought Elaine. Probably six yards. Three new players. Well, two . . . and a nine-year-old.

Just before they restarted another kid arrived. He was big. Looked about fourteen. Soon as Elaine saw him she thought: If only he's able to kick a ball – just stand there and hoof it up the pitch – he'd be tailormade for a centre-half.

'What age are you?'

'Twelve.'

'Twelve, when?'

41

'Third of August.'

Three days underage!

'Ever play before?'

'Gaelic football.'

'Who for?'

'Éire Og.'

'How come you were never down here before?'

'I was never asked.'

'Who asked you?'

'Jake Flynn.'

'Did he promise you anything?'

'No, just asked me to come down.'

'Think you can play centre-half?'

'Course I can. There's a bit of a problem though.'

'What?'

'I don't know the rules.'

They would have to teach him the rules! Easy!

Then one of the two newly arrived ex-Dublin players said to Elaine, 'Do you play much football yourself?' He had good reason to ask. Elaine looked really snazzy in her Sky Blues Coventry football strip. She smiled and said, 'Mickey Gynn used to wear this jersey. Ever hear tell of Mickey Gynn?'

'No.'

'Coventry City only won the FA Cup once. This is the same jersey Mickey Gynn wore in the final.'

Elaine had the Sky Blue knicks and socks as well.

Maybe Mickey Gynn had worn them too.

Her boots were Puma, usual low-cut style, but with good ankle support. If she could play half as well as she looked, she'd be some player.

'What can you do with a ball?' asked the ex-Dub.

'Oh, almost anything that can be done.'

Elaine took one of the practice balls and solo bounced it off her knee a few times, let it drop on to the angle of her foot, flicked it back on to her knee and repeated the action this time with her other foot. She repeated the action ten or fifteen times.

'Can anyone else do that?'

'I can,' said one of the ex-Dubs, 'but I can only do it with my right foot.'

'Can anyone do it with both feet?'

The nine-year-old stepped forward. He stuck the remains of his lollipop in his tracksuit pocket, took the ball from Elaine and repeated the procedure, no bother; solo bounced the ball off his knee a few times, transferred the ball on to the angle of his foot, juggled it a few times and flicked the ball up on to his knee, transferred the action to his left knee and repeated the procedure.

'The Lollipop Kid,' murmured Gavin's brother.

'What?'

'The Lollipop Kid. We'll call him the "Lollipop Kid".'

The kid liked that. He beamed. He looked as pleased as if he'd scored a goal for Man United. 'Lollipop Kid' sounded cool. A great nickname for an U-9 playing U-12 football.

'What part of Greystones are you from?' asked Elaine. She hadn't seen the Lollipop Kid around before. None of them had. Maybe he was a stranger, on holidays or something.

'Trafalgar Road. My Mammy's only moved out here. We used to live in Dundrum.'

'Did you play for anyone out there?'

'I was in a street-league. And then I joined Rosemount.'

'Did you ever play for them?'

'No, my Mammy wouldn't let me. Then we left and came to Greystones because my Granny's not well and my Mammy has to look after her.'

'Did you sign a form for Rosemount?'

'No. Only for the street-league. We played against Mulvey Park and teams from near the Bottle Tower and Windy Arbour.'

Lar Holmes and Elaine were impressed. The kid had

potential. Still, it remained to be seen how he could play under match conditions.

They started a practice match. Elaine refereed, while Lar Holmes watched, trying to puzzle out which positions would suit the players best. They could have done with a few friendly matches against other teams before the season started. It would have been much easier to determine players' potential playing positions under real match conditions, rather than while playing in what was little better than a kick-about. But Lar had only just been reinstated with Shamrock Boys. Most teams they knew were already booked out with friendlies.

The Lollipop Kid was certainly something special. He could take on players and beat them, spray the ball about with pin-point accuracy. And he was fast. He had a humdinger of a shot – more akin to that of a twelve-year-old. Jake had unearthed a real find in the Lollipop Kid. Without a doubt he would be the team's star turn, their match-winner, their ace-in-the-hole.

The two ex-Dubs said they had two years' league experience under their belts with Rivermount Boys from Finglas. Already Lar Holmes was contemplating using one of them at the centre of the defence with the Éire Og Gaelic player. The Gaelic player wasn't bad. He was quick and strong, with a good thump out of a ball. He was reasonably skilled and mustard keen. He'd do. A little extra coaching, a brush-up on the rules and a few league matches behind him and he'd be as good as was required. Maybe they wouldn't play the Lollipop Kid wide on the right after all. Maybe they'd play him centre midfield. He certainly looked well capable of playing there. Gavin's brother, Gary, was a good player. A goalscorer.

They were still a few players short, though. With some luck, what was needed might just ramble into the Railway Field in the next few weeks. Kids were always slow getting into the swing of things at the start of the football season.

44

They usually didn't become aware that the season had begun, not until the English League fixtures started on TV. Maybe Jake would unearth another star turn in the same mould as the Lollipop Kid? Not a chance!

After the training session Elaine and Lar discussed their plans for the team and some of their own personal aspirations.

Lar spoke with a deep feeling of sincerity in his voice. 'I hope the team's in Dublin. I've always wanted Dublin football. I've never run a team in Dublin before.'

'Never?'

'Twenty years runnin' football teams . . . never played in Dublin. I've lost cups and leagues, had good players leave and players poached. I only had one half-decent team in all the years I put into football. And that was only because Gavin and Hammer were involved. Then, I blew it. I don't want the same thing to happen again. Glad to have you help out, Elaine.'

'You love football, don't you, Lar?'

'Yes. I guess I grew up on it.'

'How's the club looking after you for gear?'

'They've given me an old set of jerseys and a few training balls. They'll hand us two match balls when we play our League matches.'

'Think they'll give us a new strip?'

'Not likely. We'll organize a raffle. A few shops'll put up prizes. I can hold the draw in one of the pubs.'

'Gavin and Hammer'd like to contribute. They said they'd send over a coaching manual and a few pounds towards the cost of a set of jerseys.'

'That's great. I'll go ahead with the raffle anyway. The extra few bob will come in handy. There's a bit of a problem, though. It's a shame not knowin' whether we're in Dublin or Wicklow. There's not many entries for the Wicklow League yet. Just us and Riverside Boys from Bray. If there's no pick-up by the middle of the week the Dublin

Schoolboys will be putting us and Riverside into Dublin. They'd place us in one of the weaker sections. It'd give us a chance to build, and maybe over a year or two turn the team into something worth having . . . How are you fixed for going to matches on Saturday mornings?'

'Saturdays don't really suit. Sometimes I play hockey. I'll be all right for training though.'

'Two nights?'

'No, one.'

'Good. I can take the second night on my own. What night suits you?'

'Tuesday. Why don't you ask Jake to give a hand? He'd love to.'

'We couldn't have him near the team. He's in trouble with the Wicklow League as it is.'

'That's only minor.'

'He's some messer.'

'Let him give a hand. He won't mess. If you're playing in Dublin you'll need someone. It's not easy, especially at home games. He could put the nets up, put down the corner-flags. Even mark the pitch in a hurry. I won't be there most Saturdays. Jake would love to help out.'

'What about his band?'

'Bands don't play Saturday mornings.'

'They rehearse, don't they?'

'Not on Saturday mornings. Don't forget Jake would get players you don't even know exist. He'd be worth having. And he does want to help.'

'Right. Maybe. But there'll have to be no messin' from him. He got this club into trouble before. And it isn't forgotten about. Tell him he can help. But he'll have to behave. No scams, no messin', no nothin'.'

'I'll do that, Lar . . . By the way, if we're put into Dublin, Riverside will hardly get in.'

'What d'ye mean?'

'Well, they play off the People's Park in Bray. There are

46

no dressing-rooms in the People's Park. You have to have dressing-rooms in the Dublin Schoolboys League.'

'That's all sorted out. If they get into Dublin they'll be using St Gerard's College as a home pitch.'

'Have they still got the Opel?'

'Yeah, Paul Glynn still uses it for transport. It's fallin' apart. Some day the whole team'll get killed in it. It's not taxed nor insured either.'

'They're always a good team. They'll be hard to beat.'

'Yeah, them and Harry Hennessy.'

'Harry Hennessy won't be doing Dublin matches. He's a Wicklow ref.'

'Maybe so. But he's on the Dublin Schoolboys list of referees. Sure as hell Harry will be out there when we play Riverside in Bray. And you don't beat Riverside Boys, not with Harry Hennessy around.'

Harry Hennessy was a demon. A demon pint-drinker; a demon referee, especially as far as visiting teams were concerned. He was also very fat; a human beer-keg who loved football and Arthur Guinness. When Harry was in form Riverside were sure to win. Riverside Boys were Harry's neighbours, and Harry was always good to his neighbours. Not that Riverside were a bad team. They were good – very good. Harry made them even better.

Elaine and Lar had spent enough time talking. It was time to get the kids out of the Railway Field and home. Lar locked the pavilion and he and Elaine walked towards the laneway at the entrance to the Railway Field.

A train thundered by on the railway embankment. Lar had seen many trains pass on the embankment over the years. To Lar, trains were just like footballers: They came, and they went.

Just like Gavin and Hammer a few years previously.

London Albion's Youths were on a winning streak, and to celebrate Glenn Thomas suggested that they should have a night out on the town without being shackled by Stevie Hodgson or Bill Thornbull. Saturday night was the most suitable as it was the only night the Youths were allowed to stay out late. The plan was to go somewhere for a quiet drink and then, perhaps, a disco afterwards. However, some of the players had second thoughts; eighteen in one group was a bit much. And going to pubs . . . most of the lads weren't into drink. Anyway, all of them were underage. They wouldn't be served. 'There's no problem . . . No problem,' assured Glenn. 'The pubs'll be glad of the business.'

Gavin had reservations. 'What if Stevie finds out?'

'He won't. Anyway we deserve a night out together.'

Arrangements were made. And on the night the Youth squad shared four taxis. They found it very hard to get into a pub, much less get served. And the reason wasn't because they were all underage, but rather because there were too many of them. In desperation Glenn went into an off-licence and bought a bottle of vodka. When he came back out he instructed the cavalcade of taxis to head for White's Hotel, Lancaster Gate.

'What's so special about White's Hotel?' asked Sandy Black.

'We'll get in there. We can order minerals and anyone who wants a drink can mix in some vodka.'

'What if they see the bottle?'

'They won't. I'll keep it hidden.'

'Hey, White's Hotel, that's where the FA go after their meetings, isn't it?'

'Sure,' leered Glenn Thomas. 'That's another reason I want to go there. I was up before the FA Disciplinary Commitee last year. I know some of the committee to see. I'll point'm out.'

'Do they know you?'

'Naw, they wouldn't remember.'

'It's Saturday night. They'd hardly be there on a Saturday night. They'd be out with their wives.'

'That lot don't have wives. They're too much into football and drinkin' pints.'

Twenty minutes later the Youths were in White's Hotel, going reasonably easy on the orange. All except Glenn Thomas, of course. He had graduated to shorts, stocked from the bottle of vodka inside his coat pocket.

'The FA, are they here?'

'There's a few. See that table over there? They're FA. The secretary is there. He was on the committee that suspended me for two matches last season.'

'What did you do?'

'I cracked a joke about the ref and he sent me off.'

'Must have been some joke.'

'It was. I'm still laughin' . . . Know what? I'm goin' to get my own back.' Glenn took a sachet of powder from his pocket – a kind of high-powered laxative. 'I was saving this up for Bill Thornbull. I think I'll give it to that secretary fella instead.'

'You wouldn't slip it into his drink?'

'I'll just wait for the right moment.'

Glenn sat back and watched what was going on at the FA table. After a few minutes a round of drinks was ordered. Glenn saw his chance and went to the bar to see that Mr Secretary got a drink to remember.

As he made a beeline for the bar Glenn passed an eagle-eye over the array of drinks at the FA table. The secretary was on water. At least it looked like water. Probably a gin and tonic. He'd hardly make a show out of the FA by socializing on water. Quite definitely, he was a gin and tonic man. The only one in the company.

'Excuse me,' said Glenn to the barman. 'A tomato juice.'

'Feeling sick?'

'No, peckish.'

The barman got Glenn the tomato juice. Then turned to look after the FA's round. Only one gin and tonic was put up on the counter. Glenn was sitting within arm's reach, and when the barman turned to put a head on a pint he unloaded the laxative into the gin and tonic and gave it a quick stir with his finger. He giddily finished his tomato juice and went back to the lads.

'It's all done. Just hope the secretary gets full value.'

'What if they suspect someone meddled with the drink?'

'They won't. They're elephants. Typical off-duty FA. No wonder football is goin' down the tubes.'

The secretary drank the gin and tonic. Fifteen minutes later he was on his way to the toilets.

'Bombs away!'

Gavin timed him. Seventeen minutes dead.

It was a real giggle.

'Let's go night-clubbing,' said Glenn.

'What if Stevie Hodgson finds out?'

'Who's to know? Stevie Hodgson ain't God. He's not goin' to know our every move. Let's have a bit of fun just for one night.'

The Youth squad filed out into the foyer of White's Hotel. Glenn intended to say goodbye to the FA secretary but he was out in the toilets on a second visit.

'We're too young to be allowed into a night-club.'

'A disco, then?'

'Yeah, a disco.'

Outside, Sandy Black stood on the edge of the road and flagged down three taxis.

'Mick, you're from London. Where's there a good disco?'

'One that doesn't serve drink,' groaned Glenn Thomas. 'I'm sick of drink.'

As soon as he had set foot outside the foyer of White's Hotel the night air had hit him like a brick wall. He felt like spewing-up. But just managed to control it.

The disco was out Brixton way. It was full of West Indians and flashing white teeth.

'Make yourselves at 'ome, lads.'

'Do we need passports?' mimicked Cyril Stevens.

The place was jammed tight, reggae music and scraggy thin pig-tails of hair.

'Mick, why did you bring us here?'

''Cause it's different.'

'It's like Kingston, Jamaica, with the lights gone out,' sputtered Glenn Thomas. 'Who's your man? Bob Marley's double?'

Glenn was really out on his feet. Totally sloshed. Still, he struggled across the disco floor, towards a constellation of sparkling lights.

Crash! He walked smash-bang through the door.

'What happened?'

'You walked through a door.'

'A door? Am I a ghost or what?'

'No, it was a glass door.'

Glenn was in trouble. They were all in trouble. The manager of the club had recognized a few of them, Mick Bates in particular. To make matters worse, he was a Crystal Palace supporter. He would take the greatest of pleasure in reporting the matter to London Albion AFC.

Straight away the manager ordered all eighteen of them from the club. It only took a few minutes to horse them out on to the street. Their egos were totally deflated – thrown out of a two-bit disco!

'Who're we playin' next week?' croaked Glenn Thomas, slumped in the back of a taxi on the return to the digs. 'I hope that FA fellow gets better. And I hope Crystal Palace gets walloped!'

It certainly had been a night to remember. But John Warner would remember it better than most once the complaints started trickling back to London Albion.

Word wasn't long in filtering back to London Albion about the Saturday night escapade. Stevie and Bill Thornbull were furious. Punishment would have to be meted out.

Surprisingly the punishment didn't consist of extra training. Instead they were brought into Brompton and handed mops and buckets of water. They had to mop the visiting team's dressing-room, the shower area and the passageway that led from the dressing-rooms out on to the pitch. They even had to clean out the toilets, including the public ones beneath the West Stand. Glenn Thomas bore the worst of the brunt. While all the others had mops he was given a hand-scrub and assigned to the part of the dressing-room most in need of attention. Then Bill Thornbull brought him to the kitchens and gave him a stint of pot-cleaning, plus another floor-scrubbing session.

'Drink's a demon,' screeched Bill Thornbull. 'Specially if it ain't handled properly. Lad, you're on the slippery slope to ruin. We don't want you to be a monk. But you gotta learn to handle yourself.'

'Yes, Bill.'

'Yes, master.'

'Yes, sir.'

Neither did Glenn escape being brought into John Warner's office and given a rollicking. He was blamed for the total misdemeanours of the Youth squad. Any more trouble, any more wild nights out on the town, and he'd be shown the door. 'Your folks wouldn't like to see that happening, would they?'

'No,' gulped Glenn.

'Remember, you have a duty to yourself, your people, and this club. That duty is to behave.'

'We were only having some fun.'

'Only having some fun! That's very lame. Pathetic. You saw what happened to Darren Blyth last season. Darren was one of the best Youth-team prospects to be produced by this club. Because he had a discipline problem we let him go. The goals have dried up on the first team at the moment. Darren would have solved that. What I'm trying to say is, no one individual is bigger than this club. Darren was shown the door. And if you can't behave you'll go the same way, FA Youths Cup prospects impaired or not.'

The message was short and to the point. Glenn had better behave, or else.

That was not the only piece of bad news for Glenn. John Warner produced a letter addressed to the club. He read it out. The tone was crisp and curt; an enclosed bill detailed the cost of replacing the glass door that Glenn had walked through.

'It'll be stopped out of your wages.'

'But . . .'

'And on top of that you're fined two weeks' wages.'

'But I need extra money next week.'

'You'll just have to go without. Learn to behave and to show a sense of responsibility. I don't want your name bein' brought to my attention again. Behave yourself in future.'

Glenn left the office in gloom. Fined two weeks' wages! And he'd have to pay for the glass door. John Warner wouldn't have to worry any more. By the time the fine and glass door were paid for he wouldn't have any money left to go and get himself into trouble.

Anyway, he didn't intend to get himself thrown out of the club like Darren Blyth. If he ever got thrown out of London Albion he'd be absolutely devastated. Football was his god. He lived for football. Who were the Youths down to play next? Charlton? That'd cheer him up. He always played well against Charlton. There was no way he was going to misbehave in future.

Drink? Who needed drink? Bill Thornbull was right when he said drink was a demon.

Glenn's heels had been cooled. He'd behave himself in future.

4

Shamrock Boys and Riverside Boys were both accepted by the Dublin District Schoolboys League. The section was made up mainly of southside teams: Mount Merrion, Valeview, Ballybrack, Carriglea Boys, St John Bosco, Crumlin Utd, Loughlinstown Utd. The northside teams were St Paul's Artane and St Kevin's 'B'. First game for Shamrock Boys was to be against St John Bosco from Drimnagh.

A few days after Lar Holmes got word that Shamrock Boys had been officially accepted by the Dublin District Schoolboys League Jake picked up another player – Éire Og's star performer. He fitted like a glove into midfield. And what was better, he already knew the rules. Jake's name was put in Éire Og's little black book. They didn't want him near the club. They regarded him as the enemy. Neither would they be going to any of Scorpion Jack's gigs. 'He's robbed us of our two best players. Him and his foreign game . . . and his foreign music.'

By now Shamrock Boys didn't intend to be just making up the numbers or propping up the bottom of the league. They had Gavin's brother, the Lollipop Kid, the two exiles from Éire Og, the ex-Rivermount duo, plus a rejuvenated squad under Elaine and Lar Holmes' tutelage. Even more encouraging, Lar was beginning to keep his mouth shut. His days of giving out and shouting at players seemed to be coming to an end.

In short, Shamrock Boys intended to be up there fighting with the top teams. They wanted to make a real go of it and give Lar Holmes and Elaine their first ever Dublin League pennant.

Lar was due to hold the draw in aid of the new football kit in a week's time. He had a good deal lined up with a fellow who worked for O'Neills of Capel Street. And already, Shamrock Boys' club committee had sanctioned the payment in advance of the league fee, and also the money for the hire of a minibus for the U-12s first league fixture away to St John Bosco. The committee didn't like it when they heard Lar had organized a raffle in the Beach House. They felt that he should have obtained the Club's permission first. Old wounds began to surface. Already there was trouble brewing between Lar and Shamrock Boys' committee.

Unknown to Lar and the Fraud Squad, Jake had been out fund-raising. He told Luke all about the escapade.

'Not a word to Lar Holmes what I'm going to tell you. He might blow a fuse. Anyway, it was all for a good cause: to help out schoolboy soccer. I made up two collection boxes from some plywood left over from the woodwork class at school. On one I wrote Riverside Boys; on the other the name of a team from Dun Laoghaire. Then I went out two nights; Friday in Bray, Sunday in Dun Laoghaire. I did all the pubs. I got sixty-three quid and the price of a bag of chips from the Bray collection; ninety quid and a hamburger from the Dun Laoghaire collection. You'd think that means people in Dun Laoghaire are more generous than people in Bray. Not really. There are two different clubs in Dun Laoghaire, both with the same name – the one I used on the Dun Laoghaire collection box. I have the money at home. I hope to hand it over to Lar soon as I see him.'

'You're supposed to have a permit to collect money.'

'So what? I was going to make up a third collection box with "For the Poor" written on it and leave it inside the chapel door for the Sunday Masses. But maybe that'd be goin' a bit too far . . . Don't go and tell Lar Holmes . . .'

'I won't.'

'He'll be happy enough once he doesn't know the full

details. What do you think about the collection?'

'Wrong. But a great laugh.'

'Just shows you. Where there's a will, there's a way.'

Jake handed over the money from the two collections to Lar Holmes at the Tuesday night training session. Lar was delighted. He thought the money was collected quite legally. A training manual and forty pounds from Gavin and Hammer had arrived in the post the day before. He wouldn't be depending on the raffle in the Beach House for a new strip. Soon as training was over he would be on the phone to his contact to ask O'Neills to have the new football strip ready for the week-end. They wouldn't be trotting out against St John Bosco in old faded jerseys. With a bit of luck they'd be wearing a flashy new strip of green and white, with tracksuits for the substitutes. Maybe O'Neills would throw in a free medical kit as a good-will gesture. There'd be no harm in asking.

The complete squad showed up for training. Elaine was also there, putting the players through their paces. There had been no moaning, no shirking. They had all got stuck in and taken the training session seriously. They seemed a good bunch of lads. Prior to training there had been only the one problem. The Lollipop Kid's mother didn't want him training at night. 'If they don't train, they don't play,' ranted Lar Holmes. Jake saved the day. He had a word with the Kid's mother. The Kid was allowed to train, but someone would have to leave him home afterwards.

The match against St John Bosco was a thriller. The ref had to work overtime. Lar Holmes was up and down the line like a yo-yo. The Lollipop Kid was brilliant. He scored a hat-trick and left the St John Bosco goalkeeper's face swollen with a shot that rebounded off his face. On the sideline one wag shouted at the goalkeeper, 'You better not tell your Ma a nine-year-old gave you tha'. She'd throw you out. Say you were over in the boxin' club and Michael Carruth gave you a thump.'

In spite of their great effort, Shamrock Boys lost 4-3. Still, Lar Holmes wasn't disappointed. The team had done well. Not one of the players had performed badly. They had given their all, and he knew he couldn't ask for any more. As for the Lollipop Kid he was something else.

Elaine's quarter-final tie in the LFAI Cup was against Benfica, a Waterford team. She had to sacrifice a few Tuesday night training sessions with Shamrock Boys U-12s, as the Brighton Celtic manager was adamant that she should attend all training sessions in preparation for the Cup game. Brighton Celtic had never got to the quarter-final of the LFAI Cup before and they were determined to give it their best shot. Luckily they were drawn at home in Cornelscourt. Home advantage was always a huge plus in a cup-tie. Brighton felt they had every chance of making the semi-final.

A few weeks before interest in the coming match reached fever pitch Elaine discovered how Jake had raised the money towards the cost of the U-12s' football gear. She wasn't too pleased. Jake casually told her about it; he thought it a great laugh. Elaine could see that he hadn't the sense to realize that what he had done was dishonest. He treated the whole thing as a joke. A bit of bravado. The police would have had a different name for it; collecting money under false pretences. Luckily they weren't aware of Jake's scam. Nobody was. Lar Holmes would have gone berserk if he had known. People could go to jail for what Jake had done.

Elaine gave him some tongue-lashing. What was he? a child of six without any awareness of what was right and what was wrong? It was time he gave up playing the joker. Time he grew up. To think he was working his butt off to put Scorpion Jack on the map and he could go out with two collection boxes and do something as stupid as he had done. If the police had latched on to him he would have been ruined. If anybody had reported him . . .! To think that he could have put his own future – and Scorpion Jack's – in jeopardy by committing such an irresponsible act. Just for a laugh! Elaine told him he was as thick as the wall to have that mentality. Gavin and Hammer were doing the best they could to get on in life. The effort that he himself put into Scorpion Jack meant he cared and wanted to be a success. But to go around Bray and Dun Laoghaire conning people out of money – that was courting disaster. It was definitely time for Jake to cop-on before it was too late.

The whole episode made Elaine seeth. Sometimes she wondered about Jake, and, to a minor degree, about Luke. He didn't seem to have any drive, any ambition – except for his pigeons. What were they? Imbeciles?

The LFAI Cup quarter-final was a two-thirty Sunday kick-off, and Brighton Celtic expected a big crowd. The perimeter of the pitch was roped off and the lines freshly marked. Benfica brought a bus load of travelling support. Brighton had all the locals, plus relatives and friends of the players. Elaine's mother and father came in from Greystones – he was really hyped-up for the game. Being an ex-pro, cup games had a special appeal for him, a sense of nostalgia. They had brought Jake in tow. He was in bouyant mood, sharing some half-truth, some half-lie with an unsuspecting spectator.

Elaine had come up from Greystones earlier in the morning. The game being such an important one the team practiced a few set-pieces first, then had lunch in a nearby hotel. After lunch the match plan was discussed, and any weaknesses of the opposition noted. They then made their way to the pitch to get ready for the game. Benfica were there before them, ready and waiting.

The game was a close affair. Nil-all at half-time. Nil-all most of the way through the second half. Elaine was playing midfield, passing the ball about with ease and confidence. Normally she played centre-forward but a friend of hers from Bray was switched into the centre-forward position for the day as Brighton felt her robustness might unsettle the Benfica defence more easily than Elaine's nimble skills. The Benfica defence was on the small side, highly skilled but not physically tough. Under the circumstances the Brighton management thought it better to play a more physical player up front and slot Elaine into an attacking midfield role. The Brighton mentors were partly right, partly wrong in their ploy. Although the replacement centre-forward was well able for the Benfica defence physically, her finishing should have been a lot sharper. She missed several good goalscoring opportunities.

Luckily for Brighton, however, Elaine was in top form. One chipped shot just out of the goalkeeper's reach came off the crossbar and was diverted wide for a corner. Another shot took a deflection and looped viciously wide of the top upright. Benfica then put Brighton under a lot of pressure. But Elaine played really well. She set up several lightning quick counter-attacks. Then Benfica put a marker on her anytime she ventured into their half of the field. Worse, they tried to deny her possession by not playing the ball in her direction. It wasn't easy going from then on in. Maybe the Brighton management should have switched her to centre-forward in the hope she could collect a few loose balls and put Brighton on the scoreboard. But tactically Brighton were clueless. The game finished nil-all. If Brighton couldn't win at home they'd hardly win away. Benfica wouldn't let them off the hook in the replay. Brighton as good as knew they were out of the Cup.

On the way back to Greystones Elaine's father told her that the Irish Ladies team manager was at the game.

Little did Elaine, or her father, realize that more than the Irish team manager was watching her. She would shortly be vetted from afar. Through his soccer connections Elaine's father was friendly with a John Hallsworth, a small-time football agent who mainly dealt with lower division English League players who, through insurance pay-offs and dead-end circumstances, were looking for an escape route into the lower realms of European football. There was never a big amount of money involved in the deals, just enough to keep the business ticking over. But he had a nice sideline going in ladies' soccer. Most of the big British agents weren't into ladies' soccer. It gave John something of a free hand.

John had seen Elaine play as a thirteen-year-old and was impressed. He put her name on file. There it would remain until – hopefully – his memory would be jogged by some future enquiry for an up-and-coming female soccer starlet.

It happened one morning early in November. John Hallsworth got to his office near the Bull Ring in Birmingham twenty minutes late. There was a message on the telex. He was pleased. A telex from Turin was always welcome. This one read:

> *Elaine Clarke. Juventus Ladies interested.*
> `*Massimo Tardelli.*

Massimo Tardelli was his Italian contact.

Elaine Clarke! How the hell had they found out about her? Maybe he had mentioned her name somewhere. Maybe the Italians had been watching her when she played locally in the Midlands before moving to Ireland. Still, who cared? Massimo Tardelli had her earmarked for Juventus. Tardelli was one to be reckoned with. He knew his job. And he was big into lira. Ireland? Elaine Clarke's Irish address wasn't on file. Easy. He'd ring Coventry City and find out where in Ireland the Clarkes had moved to.

Coventry City hadn't a clue. They had no idea where in Ireland Elaine's father was. John Hallsworth then rang the Clarkes old address at Regent Street, Coventry. Terrible!

The Clarkes hadn't left a forwarding address.

He rang Massimo Tardelli in Turin.

'John Hallsworth speaking, Mr Tardelli. Elaine Clarke has gone to live in Ireland. I don't have an address for her.'

'Work on it. Ask around.'

'I have. No one seems to know. Mr Tardelli, Elaine Clarke is very young. Maybe too young.'

'How young is young?'

'Seventeen.'

'Seventeen is not so young. By next season she will be eighteen. We wanna look at her in summer. Turin in mid-June. Juventus are in the business of wanting her. Can you make the approach?'

'Yes, if I can find her address.'

'Find her. This is many lira deal.'

John Hallsworth went back to the computer file. Elaine's ex-football club: No phone number. Ex-school: Bingo!

'My name is John Hallsworth. I'm trying to check out an Elaine Clarke. She went to your school until two years ago. Her family moved to Ireland. I was wondering if you, or any of the pupils, would have an address for her?'

'I'll see. Could you ring back after the lunchtime break?'

'What time is that?'

'Anytime after two.'

John rang back at two-fifteen.

'One of the girls has an address: Hillview, Applewood Heights, Greystones, County Wicklow.'

'Do you have a phone number?'

'Sorry, no. Why don't you ring directory Enquiries in Ireland?'

John did that. He got Elaine's phone number.

Good-bye, athletics.

Good-bye, Brighton Celtic.

5

The 'D' section of the Dublin Schoolboys League went reasonably well for Shamrock Boys. After eight matches they had dropped four points; two points to St John Bosco and another two points away to Mount Merrion. The team had gelled satisfactorily, with the two Éire Og players taking to soccer like ducks to water. Also, the ex-Rivermount duo were very experienced players who lent a steadying influence to the team. The guide-rule from Lar Holmes on the sideline was – if under pressure give the ball to the Rivermount duo. Both were as cool as cucumbers and could hold the ball if need be, especially Ray in midfield. The other half of the duo was Ken, but being a centre-half it wasn't advisable for him to hold the ball for too long. But he wasn't one for getting ruffled and always played the ball cleverly out of defence.

Gavin's brother, Gary, was also playing well. He was the team's top scorer. But the team's star performer, as ever, was the Lollipop Kid. Already Lar Holmes was coming under pressure to let him play on Shamrock Boys U-9 team.

'Under-twelve is a bit much. He could get broke up. Let him play under-nine.'

But Lar wouldn't allow it. He obstinately refused.

'Not bloody likely.'

Nine matches into the season and Shamrock Boys were down to play Riverside Boys at home in the Railway Field. Jake made sure he was there. Unfortunately Brighton Celtic had called a training session for the same time as the Riverside fixture. Brighton Celtic's replay in the LFAI Cup against Benfica from Waterford was due the next day and they wanted to work on deadball situations in advance of the game. As Elaine took most of Brighton Celtic's free kicks she had no choice but to miss the Riverside game and attend training.

Any tie between Shamrock Boys and Riverside was sure to be full of incident and one to savour. Riverside were drawn mainly from the Dargle area of Bray. Traditionally they were all very good footballers, if somewhat wild. The present crop of players, under the stewardship of manager Mr Glynn, were no exception. Mr Glynn still had the same Opel estate car as when Gavin and Hammer used to play for Shamrock Boys. It now had more dents and scratches and the engine roared louder. But its pulling power hadn't diminished in the slightest. Twelve to fourteen kids piled one on top of the other wasn't enough to constitute a problem for the engine, whatever about the suspension. But then the car's suspension didn't exist any more, so the question didn't arise.

Riverside Boys usually met on the Lower Dargle Road for away matches. As soon as Mr Glynn's car appeared there was always a mad charge – though last in always got the best seats. Best seats were on top, beside the windows. That way their heads, at least, wouldn't get squashed. They could always open the windows, stick their heads out and shout a few remarks (abusive or otherwise) to passers-by.

'Hey, Mister, is the dog bringin' you for a walk?'

'What's your name, Mister? Bonzo?'

'Woof! Woof!'

Riverside had had a bad experience the week before the Shamrock Boys fixture and as a result there was a rumour going around among the players which possibly would affect morale for the trip to Greystones in Mr Glynn's Opel. The week before had been a home fixture and the visiting manager had felt weak. He half collapsed. Mr Glynn had put him into his car and brought him to St

Columcille's Hospital, Loughlinstown, where he was kept in overnight. They released him as fit and healthy the next day.

'Where's David Roche?'

'He's not comin'. Says he's goin' to no matches in a hearse.'

'What do you mean?'

'Says that man you took to hospital last week died in the back of the car and he ain't goin' to no matches in the back of a hearse.'

'Nobody died in the back of the car.'

'You're lyin', Mr Glynn.'

'Nobody died. The man is all right. He was discharged from hospital the next day.'

'That's a pity. Some of us were hopin' the car'd be haunted. None of us ever seen a ghost before.'

Mr Glynn felt exasperated. He tied their football bags to the Opel's roof-rack and piled the last of the players into the car. All except two who had brought a black mongrel with them.

'You can't bring that dog!'

'Mr Glynn, he won't take up much room. He's small.'

'He could bite someone.'

'He likes lookin' out car windows. Mr Glynn, he'll be real quiet if he sits near the window.'

'He isn't coming. Bring him out to Greystones and he'll probably spend the whole time running after the ball. He'd ruin the match.'

'Lock him in the car.'

'Not likely. You'll just have to leave him where he is.'

The two boys looked crestfallen.

'Mr Glynn, me mother'll murder me if I don't bring the dog.'

'Let her. Get into the car.'

They released the dog and got into the car.

One of the kids, Bonkers O'Toole, yelped from the back

of the car. 'Never mind the dog. You're lucky you got a mammy. Mine dumped me in a railway station in Birmingham when I was seven. I never saw her since.'

'I wonder why?' sighed Mr Glynn.

'Talkin' of mammies,' said Lucky Burke, the Riverside Boys' outside-left, 'Mine left me outside the toilets at the Town Hall when I was one-and-a-half.'

'There's no toilets at the Town Hall.'

'There was when I was one-and-a-half.'

'Mr Glynn, the dog . . .'

'Nobody remembers when they were one-and-a-half.'

'I do. Me Mammy went into the toilets and forgot to put the brake on the pram. The pram took off down the Main Street. I was lucky I wasn't hit by a car. When me Ma came out of the toilets she was in an awful state.'

'Where did you end up?'

'In a smashed shop window, sittin' on a lump of ham.'

'Mr Glynn, Madra's scratchin' at the car door.'

'Who's Madra?'

'The dog.'

'What?'

'He's scratchin' at the door.'

Mr Glynn gave in. The dog was quickly bundled into the car and the Opel Estate headed up the Dargle Road towards Main Street; then the Vevay and the open road towards Greystones.

Riverside Boys usually sang a few songs on the trip to away fixtures. Their favourite was 'You'll Never Walk Alone'. They they had 'Nice one, Cyril . . . Nice one, son . . . Nice one, Cyril . . . Let's have another one'. For the trip to Greystones they sang 'Nice one, Cyril', only they substituted Madra for Cyril and they sang the song over and over in the hope that Madra would break wind. But he wasn't a very obedient dog. He failed to oblige.

The interior of Mr Glynn's car was well documented with the autographs of many present and ex-Riverside players, amongst them one Chopper Doyle, who recently had taken over the People's Park in Bray with an old, old nag he called a racehorse. He left it hobbled in the Park at night and was back during the day to gallop and jump it over a few obstacles he made up from some debris he had taken from the river that skirted the Park. Most lads weren't sure whether Chopper was in training to be a jockey, a stuntman or a cowboy – or all three. One certainty, nobody could walk in safety in the Park during the day, not with Chopper and his horse around. It was just as well Riverside's U-12s played their home matches in St Gerard's.

Both Chopper and his horse were far from the minds of Riverside as they sped down Windgates towards the Railway Field. The sing-song was going well. Just as strong as the wind whistling through the football gear on the roof-rack. And Madra sitting upright, cradled in one of the team's laps, was having a good look at the countryside.

They got to the Railway Field with about a quarter of an hour to spare. For Riverside's U-12s it was their first-ever visit to the Railway Field. They were impressed, more so with the dressing-rooms than with the pitch.

'It's got showers, Mr Glynn.'

'So what? So has St Gerard's.'

'The water's hot, Mr Glynn. Can we have a shower before we go out on the pitch? It might help loosen us up.'

Mr Glynn flatly refused the idea of a pre-match shower. They'd all forget about the match and cause pandemonium.

'Where's Lucky Burke?'

'Maybe we left him in Bray?'

'Naw, he was in the back of the car. He tried to pinch 50p outa me pocket.'

Two of the players were fighting over a jersey. Mr Glynn gave them a half-hearted clip on the ear and sorted out the problem.

'Mr Glynn, Lucky's in the showers, givin' Madra a wash.'

Mr Glynn went into the showers. Sure enough Lucky was there under a steaming hot shower, stripped off to his football knicks, lacquered in soap and giving Madra a thorough scrubbing.

'What do you think you're doing, Lucky?'

'Givin' Madra a good wash, Mr Glynn. He's got fleas. They were jumpin' all over me in the car.'

'Get in there to the dressing-room. The game's starting in a few minutes. Are they your knicks?'

'No. They're me underpants. They're cut-price ones. Me Ma got them in a sale. What'll I do with Madra?'

'Leave him. I'll look after him.'

As soon as Lucky left the showers Mr Glynn tried to grab Madra. But Madra darted out through the door and into the corridor, where he made straight for the main entrance. Mr Glynn chased after the saturated mongrel. The last he saw of him was outside on the pitch, giving himself a good shake, then he disappeared up the sideline and went through a gap in the wire-netting behind the top goal. There were some houses across the way. No doubt Madra was headed that way on the lookout for some canine company. Mr Glynn had enough of chasing dogs. He went back into the dressing-room, passing Lar Holmes on the way. Neither of them had anything to say. They ignored one another. They had had too many run-ins in the past to be on talking terms. Years of hostility, protests and counter-protests had blunted their admiration for one another. Theirs was a war situation. One just didn't converse with the enemy.

Everything out on the pitch was in great shape. The nets were up, the corner flags in place, the pitch marked to a tee. Jake had seen to it all. He had even pumped the match ball and opened the dressing-rooms for the visiting team. Other than that he was keeping in the background, minding his own business. He didn't want to get too involved. Lar Holmes and Mr Glynn were capable of causing enough trouble without any help from him. He'd leave it to the 'Old Masters' and take a back seat for a change.

Before the game had even started Riverside were on to a winner. Harry Hennessy was down to ref. He had travelled from Bray out to Greystones on the bus, the official referee's card in his jacket pocket. The sight of Harry Hennessy – all eighteen stone of him – coming into the Railway Field didn't give Lar Holmes any great pleasure. Lar knew by the time the final whistle went Shamrock Boys would be a beaten side. Sadly, whatever about Riverside, Harry Hennessy was unbeatable.

The match went as Lar Holmes predicted, the winning goal was scored from an off-side position. Jake had flagged. Harry Hennessy ignored the flag and gave the goal. Lar Holmes went bananas. The ball had been played through from the right. The Riverside centre-forward was at least two yards off-side when the ball was played. He could see that Harry Hennessy was in the other half of the field having a breather, so he just kept going, brought the ball under control and placed it wide of the Shamrock Boys' goalkeeper. When he turned he saw Jake with the linesman's flag up indicating off-side. But Harry Hennessy pointed to the centre-circle and the goal stood. Riverside had the game as good as wrapped up.

Jake tried to quieten Lar Holmes down, but it wasn't easy. Lar had, to put it mildly, blown a fuse. It took Jake quite a few minutes to calm the situation.

On the other line, Mr Glynn smiled. Riverside had Lar Holmes and Shamrock Boys on the run. Not a bad team though, Shamrock Boys. Much better than Mr Glynn expected. The little fellow anchoring midfield was good. The Lollipop Kid they were calling him. The big centre-half wasn't bad either. A bit big for an U-12. Looked overage. It would be worth banging in a protest if Riverside lost. Shamrock Boys had three or four useful players. Players that Mr Glynn wouldn't mind having. Maybe if Lar Holmes got up to his old habit of shouting at them Shamrock Boys might break up and it would leave Riverside with a chance of grabbing a few displaced players on the rebound. Gavin's brother was good too. Mr Glynn wouldn't mind having him as well. If Shamrock Boys ever broke up he'd go looking for the players he fancied – turn Riverside into a real class team. One with 'A' section potential. It'd be nice to play against the likes of Home Farm, Belvedere, Cherry Orchard, St Kevin's, St Joseph's, Stella Maris. And the way Harry Hennessy habitually favoured Riverside, they'd probably slaughter the top Dublin teams – at least at home.

Madra hadn't been seen since the kick-off. But he showed up with about ten minutes to go. Like most dogs that attended football matches he gave chase after the ball, and turned the last few minutes into a fiasco. At first, Harry Hennessy refused to take action, thinking that the dog would go away. But Madra persisted and he had to stop the game, in the hope that one of the players would grab the dog and get him off the pitch. But all was in vain.

'Damned dog,' roared Harry Hennessy.

'Damned dog' sounded familiar to Madra. So did Harry Hennessy. The estate where Madra lived in Bray was just up the road from the Dargle river and most week-ends during the football season this fat, oversized man would pass through the estate, a football bag under his arm. Usually he had a good few drinks on him, the consequence of having drunk the fees from the matches he had refereed that day. When the dogs saw him coming they usually barked. The man would always shout back 'Damned dogs', and, of course, the man was Harry Hennessy.

So when Harry shouted 'Damned dog!' in the middle of

the Railway Field familiarity grew to contempt as far as Madra was concerned. First, he growled. Then he bit Harry Hennessy's leg. It wasn't much of a bite, just a nip. But it made Harry Hennessy scream. 'Damned dog!'

Lucky Burke came on the scene, grabbed Madra and locked him up in Mr Glynn's car. Meanwhile Harry Hennessy was given some medical attention. He'd have to go to St Colmcille's Hospital in Loughlinstown after the match for a tetanus injection. There'd be no after-match bevy in his local pub back in Bray. Instead he'd be cooped-up in the casualty department of Loughlinstown Hospital. For posterity, Mr Glynn treated Harry Hennessy for Madra's bite. Lar Holmes flatly refused to do so. Harry always looked after Riverside, so let Riverside look after Harry in his hour of need. Anyway, that was Lar Holmes's attitude.

Riverside won the match nil-one. They were cock-a-hoop. Still unbeaten. Maximum points. Only one other team in the section had maximum points – Carriglea from Monkstown. Riverside were due to play them at home in a few weeks. They were unbeatable at home, so they'd be sure to give Carriglea a stuffing.

On the way back to Bray in the Opel one of the Riverside players said to Mr Glynn, 'Mr Glynn, why does Harry Hennessy always give us off-side goals?'

'. . . Because he feels he's one of us.'

'Gee, Mr Glynn, that's nice, real nice.'

Straight away, everyone in the car burst into one of their favourite songs, 'Nice one, Harry . . . Nice one, son . . . Nice one, Harry . . . Let's have another one.'

That is, all except Madra, of course.

Brighton Celtic's LFAI quarter-final Cup replay went badly for Brighton, and they went 2-0 down after fifteen minutes. They took a long time to settle. A combination of the long coach journey and hanging around Benfica's pitch waiting for the opposition to show up didn't help matters. The pitch wasn't to their liking either. It was a lot bigger than they preferred. Benfica were a very skilled and fast-moving side; the big pitch suited them perfectly. Brighton were on to a roasting.

After the second goal Elaine was pushed forward from midfield into an out-and-out striker's role. She clipped the top of the upright with a right-footed pile-driver. Luckily she was one of the few Brighton Celtic players who could match the Benfica players for pace. Her probings up front and her skill at shielding the ball helped to take some of the pressure off the defence.

After the first twenty minutes Brighton settled. They began to come into the game. Benfica began to get caught out on the counter-attack. The standard of play was of a very high order, especially from Benfica. Mostly the emphasis was on skill and ground football, a complete contrast to the over-physical and up in the air football ('moon football') that usually predominates in adult male football. Just before half-time Elaine's school-pal from Bray rounded the Benfica goalkeeper and slotted the ball into the back of the net: 2-1.

The score remained the same for most of the second half. Benfica swamped the Brighton goal but the Brighton goalkeeper was in great form. Benfica just couldn't get the better of her: one-handed tips around the post, point-blank saves, the ball taken safely out of the air from corners – it was all the same to her. She was unbeatable. At the opposite end of the pitch Elaine missed two great chances from close in. Still 2-1 for Benfica. With ten minutes to go the Brighton manager made a double substitution. It was panic stations. Somehow they just had to claw a goal back. Three minutes left and Brighton got a direct free on the edge of the Benfica penalty-area. Elaine fluffed the kick. It came back off the wall. There was a scramble and the ball fell to the rangy Brighton inside-left. She looked up. Wham! The ball struck the back of the Benfica net: 2-2. Brighton were lucky to be still in with a chance of winning the game.

The game went into extra time. Brighton ended up with one of the fulls hobbling. Benfica totally dominated. But, even yet, the Brighton goalkeeper was performing heroics. She held Benfica at bay. In the end, Brighton lost 5-4 on a penalty shoot-out.

The Ladies midwinter break was due soon. The league would not start up again until late spring. All the way back to Dublin the Brighton players had a dead, end-of-season feeling. Out of the Cup and not much hope of finishing in the top four in the League. Already they felt as if their season was at an end. If only they had beaten Benfica. If only they had gone on to win the Cup . . .

When it came to commitment and reading a game Mick Bates was the best player on London Albion's Youth team. For tackling, there was very little between Hammer, Glenn Thomas and Mick Bates. Fastest player was probably John Palmer. Craftiest player, Cyril Stevens. But for all-round ability and sticking the ball in the back of the net Numero Uno was Gavin.

Gavin oozed class. Unlike a lot of quality players he trained very hard. He didn't drink or smoke. It was the same with Hammer. Both were perfect examples of how footballers should behave. They had a great attitude towards the game. Both came back to Highfield most afternoons for extra training. Gavin was for ever working on improving his skills, trapping the ball, timing passes and runs into the box, shooting, heading and working on his dribbling skills. He put great emphasis on ball control. He believed in taking on the opposition, without being over-greedy, and going around them. He liked to run at a defence. There weren't many players plying their trade in the English League, or the Premiership, who were willing or capable of taking on a defence head-to-head. In the modern game, too much reliance was put on playing the ball into space, rather than using the exciting spectacular of dribbling skills to open a defence. In that sense Gavin was one of a dying breed. Not that he wasn't a good passer of the ball, or capable of delivering a telling pass. He was excellent on both counts. Apart from dribbling skills, shooting right or left foot was all the same to Gavin: dead ball, on the volley, on a cross from the wing, or a through-ball through the middle. Wham! He had goalscoring down to a fine art. Even with his back to goal he could judge where the goalposts were by using the markings of the penalty-area, or the centre-circle, as a guideline. It was impossible to knock him off a ball. He could trap, turn and swivel, and power a rocket of a shot for the top corner, or just inside the bottom upright. His heading ability was equally as spectacular.

He'd been over in Ireland the previous week (unfortunately Hammer hadn't been selected) playing against Romania in a European Youths qualifying game. Ireland had drawn 1-1, and Gavin had scored the Irish goal with a powerful twenty-yard header. Old-timers said it was one of the best-headed goals ever seen in Dalymount Park. And although Dalymount was well past its hey-day it had witnessed many top-class matches and humdingers of goals over the years. To say that Gavin's goal against Romania was one of the best headed goals ever seen was certainly complimentary.

Gavin's current form with London Albion was unbelievable. Stevie Hodgson wasn't finding it easy to keep the fact under wraps. Newspaper reporters were hanging around the training ground like bees around a honey-pot. They were something of a nuisance factor. Stevie consulted with John Warner. Straight away John Warner got in touch with the sports editors of the various newspapers involved.

'Lay off the kid. Either that or there'll be a blanket ban on reporters carrying out interviews with all London Albion players or staff. That includes the first-team squad.'

'You couldn't do that, John. It'd be turning down free publicity.'

'If you don't lay off the Youth team I will do it.'

That ended the nuisance of reporters and photographers pestering the Youth-team squad. John Warner had a way of handling the British Press. As with football, he was always one step ahead of the posse.

Life was certainly on the up-and-up for Gavin: on a professional contract, the star turn on the Youth team, current Irish Youth international, the most highly rated Youth prospect to be produced by London Albion in years. But he didn't let it all go to his head. He kept it all in perspective.

Poor Hammer wasn't quite on the same high road towards success. He hadn't made the Irish Youth team. He'd been dropped for two matches by Stevie Hodgson. And whereas Gavin was on a professional contract, and sending money home to help out his parents, the wage Hammer was getting as an apprentice was minimal, barely enough for him to exist on. He wasn't in a position to send money home. In a way that was what upset him most, the fact that Gavin was in a position to send money home and he had nothing. It wasn't that he felt jealous. It was just – well . . . it wasn't easy to explain.

Although Hammer had been dropped for two matches that didn't get to him. Everyone was dropped at one time or another. It was part and parcel of the game. The main thing was to get back on the team as quickly as possible. And Hammer had done just that. As regards not getting on the Irish Youth team, that was a different matter entirely.

'You'll get on the team soon,' said Gavin. 'It's just that they're not ready for you yet.'

'Not ready? How come?'

'Yeah. You weren't capped at schoolboy level. They just need to be given time to wake up to the fact that you exist.'

'But I was watched last season when I played for St Joseph's.'

'They were just keeping you in mind. One of maybe thirty players that wouldn't get a look-in. They'll let you progress a little longer over here, then bring you in.'

'Think so?'

'Course. Anyway you've another year to go at Youth level. Don't worry.'

'I'm not worried.'

'Why'd you ask me then?'

'Maybe I just want to be reassured, Gavin, that's all.'

'Hammer, you're good enough. You'll get your Youth cap. Just sit back and let it come. It'll happen. Full-time trainin' at Highfield'll make all the difference.'

'Think so?'

'I know so.'

Talking of Highfield and training: lately the Youths had been integrated with the first team and reserves during training. Sometimes the Youths got to play football with the first team, and maybe have a brief chat in the dressing-rooms after training. Being around the first-team squad – some of the top stars in the English game – gave the Youths a great boost. Often before training at Highfield the fan mail would be handed out by one or other of the coaches. (At London Albion's stadium in Brompton the girls in the office would send it down to the dressing-rooms). Most of the first team regularly got fan mail; a few of the reserves did; there was usually none for the Youths. It would have been considered a miracle for a Youth-team player to receive fan mail.

One Monday morning the miracle happened; Gavin received a letter from a fan.

'What's in it?' taunted Sandy Black. 'A demand to pay the dog licence?'

'No, it's fan mail,' retorted Gavin pulling the letter away from Sandy.

'Let's see it.'

'Give off.'

Next thing, they were all around Gavin. All except Mick Bates. He wasn't into fan mail. Once he had received an abusive letter. It had finished him with fan mail. He wasn't interested any more.

'Gavin, what's in the letter?'

'It's an invitation to a party.'

'Great! What about bringing us lot?'

'Don't think you'd be interested,' laughed Gavin, putting the invitation inside his jacket pocket. 'It's a kids' party. Twins. They're seven next week. Want to go, Glenn?'

'Not bloody likely. We get nothin'. The Arsenal and Spurs gang gets loads of letters from girls askin' them out on dates. What do we get? One snifflin' letter from two seven-year-olds askin' us to their birthday party. It ain't fair. We should be gettin' loads of letters from girls.'

'Maybe we do. Bill Thornbull probably burns'm. He doesn't like girls.'

'And they don't like him. Come on, let's get out and do some trainin'. Maybe we'll find a few girls in the bushes.'

Highfield had outdoor and indoor training facilities. The Youths liked indoor the best – the routine wasn't as strenuous – except when Bill Thornbull put them on weight training in the gym. Other than that indoor was mainly five-a-side football, tactics or a lie-in on the physiotherapist's couch for some infra-red treatment on an injury, faked or otherwise.

'I've got an injury, Bill.'

'Where?'

'Down there.'

'That's your toe. You jokin'?'

'No. It's injured.'

'Pull the other one. Get outa here! Six laps of Highfield. And when you finish don't forget the come back.'

Highfield was more like a gigantic park than a training-ground. The Youths knew every square inch of its outdoor spaces. They seemed to spend most of their time running around the place, much more so than the first team or reserves. The five-a-side football matches were like a holiday in Hawaii compared to Bill's antics of making the Youths run marathons around Highfield.

For the five-a-sides the teams were usually mixed: a sprinkling of first teamers, reserves and Youths on each team. If you were unlucky enough you could end up with a mix of the coaching staff, even Stevie Hodgson or John Warner. If you were really unfortunate you could end up with Bill Thornbull playing against you. He was an animal of a player – he'd cripple the whole Premiership if given a chance. He was only allowed to play five-a-side once in a blue moon, and in his stocking feet at that.

Once Gavin had asked him, 'Ever play League football, Bill?'

'A little.'

'Who's the best outside-left you ever played against?'

'Georgie Best.'

'Aye,' joked Sandy Black. 'And Bill's got his left foot at home to prove it.'

'None of that, you Irish ninny.'

'Temper! Temper, Bill.'

Sometimes during five-a-sides they'd run a blitz tournament. The players would pool some money and the outright winners would take all. It was a great supplement to an apprentice's wage-packet if on a winning team. But one of the lesser-known apprentices had his own supplementary benefit scam.

One of the Youths' tasks was to set up the portable

goalposts and corner-flags before five-a-side games began. Another task was to go around Highfield after training and bring in any loose balls that were lying about. This particular apprentice had a habit of hiding a few balls in the bushes that dotted the park. He'd come back after training, collect the balls and sell them to some of the Sunday league teams that played in the parks. But occasionally he had an even more profitable scam. He'd take a ball and get the Youth squad to sign the first team's signatures on the ball, then go to the pubs and auction the ball off to the highest bidder. That was his master scam – his top-rate of supplementary benefit.

Somewhere along the line, Syd Davison, the kit-man, noticed that footballs were disappearing. Naturally the Youths, being kids, and grossly underpaid, were under suspicion. He got in touch with Bill Thornbull.

'Who took the balls?' roared Bill.

'What balls?'

'The balls we use in trainin'. Twelve balls went missin' in the last two weeks. Who's got'm?'

'Maybe they fell down a rabbit-hole.'

'Who said that?'

No reply.

Bill looked down the line of players to see who was smirking.

'Maybe Tottenham Hotspur took them.'

Bill's eyes darted for a second time along the line of holier-than-thou countenances of the Youth squad. 'Right then,' he fumed, 'eight laps of Highfield.'

No more footballs disappeared from London Albion's training ground at Highfield. Ball-rustling was a thing of the past. Supplementary benefit was dead.

Although life, at times, was a load of laughs for the Youth team, mostly it was deadly serious. Some of the English-born players lived at home and came in for training and matches. They were mainly London players who had been with the club on associated schoolboy forms since they were twelve. But for those like Gavin and Hammer, who lived further afield, it wasn't easy to settle in such a vast and strange city as London. They were on their own, totally cut off from family and friends.

Kids took so much for granted when living at home. It took a lot of soul-searching to stick it out. Going away and putting down new roots could devastate many of them. It wasn't easy to persevere. At times it seemed much more inviting to go back home and give a career in football a miss. There was nothing as bad for Gavin and Hammer as sitting in Mrs Burtinshaw's living–room on a dreary winter's Sunday afternoon with the rain trickling in thin streams on the window-pane. That was the worst time of all. At least when they were at Highfield or Brompton they were involved. But away from football they felt empty and lonesome. Even studying for the GCSEs didn't mean much to them. GCSE: it sounded alien, a nonentity.

The grim reality for Gavin and Hammer and, perhaps some of the other apprentices, was that there was nothing to go home to: no job prospects, no real future. Once they left home they were on their own. It was hard. It was tough. They only had themselves to depend on. At first, it was like being on a survival course. They would either perish or flourish. Almost overnight they matured mentally. It would never have happened so readily at home: life was too easy-going. Being away from home only added to their motivation.

Oddly the person the Youths drew most comfort from when the going got rough was Syd Davison, the kit-man. 'Bear-up and grin,' was always his advice. 'There's no use in worryin'. It'll only get the better of you.'

Syd Davison was worth listening to. He always had a word for the apprentices, especially if things weren't working out as planned.

He was a permanent fixture around the place, having been on the club's books for years. He had seen players, managers, trainers and coaches come and go – the changes ring in. He had played for the reserves in the old W-M formation days. Although his job was only to look after the kit, see to the boots, have the practice and match balls ready, he was a big help, a decided asset as far as the Youths were concerned. Without him a lot of them would never have survived the rigours of London Albion. It only took a few kind words of encouragement from him to heal all the self-doubt, the homesickness, the fear of not making the grade and being rejected.

There wasn't a lot the Youths could do in appreciation, except to say, 'Thanks, Syd.'

Scorpion Jack were invited to play at Bray Community College's Hallowe'en Dance. Jake, Kev and Dave went to school there and, like Luke, who went to St. David's in Greystones (St David's was Jake's old school), they were all in Fifth Year.

The lads were really looking forward to the gig in the school hall, that is, all except Liam, the drummer. He was allergic to schools. Didn't like them in the slightest. He had dropped out at Junior Cert level and devoted his life to the memory of Keith Moon, pop music in general and the art of drum-playing. His vocation was made all the easier due to the fact that his parents were weird hippy-types left over from the 1960s. In the intervening years their minds had gone the same way as their morals. They didn't find Liam hard to control. They just didn't know he existed.

Scorpion Jack hadn't given the matter a second thought when Mr Murray, the maths teacher, asked them to play at the dance. It was only on the night that they realized they were letting themselves in for more than they were bargaining for. They had to organize the fruit and vegetable van to pick up the amplifiers and stage-props from Kev's father's factory storeroom; Scorpion Jack always rehearsed in the store-room and kept their equipment there. Unfortunately, after the amplifiers, instruments and props had been brought into the college hall, Ger Sloane, the owner of the van, forgot to lock the side door. During the dance some First Years got into the van and helped themselves to a box of apples, a sack of monkey-nuts, some pears and a half box of bananas. First anyone knew of the theft was half way through the gig when the apple butts began to fly and Mr Murray and a few more ended up on the broad of their backs due to the prevalence of banana skins bordering the dance floor.

Scorpion Jack got a bit of a slagging when they first came on stage. It wasn't easy playing in front of your schoolmates. The critics stood around the walls of the hall, sniggering and passing a few caustic remarks. To the crowd they were plain old Jake, Dave and Kev from Fifth Year. And as for the clothes they were wearing! Everybody knew Jake was wild, but as for the other three ... They were all dressed up to the nines: real heavy leather gear with bits and pieces of chains hanging off them like tinsel off a Christmas-tree. And the drummer, whoever he was, was freaked out altogether. He wore a sleeveless leather jacket with an open front. He was absolutely covered with elastoplast and bandages on his forehead, on the barrel of his arms, and across the broad of his chest. His hair went straight up like greasy clogged spikes, and he had large circles of paint splotched on his trousers. A profusion of safety-pins added glitter.

'Who're you?' shouted one of the crowd. 'Florence Nightingale's brother?'

'No,' he shouted back. 'A kidney and heart transplant patient.'

It took about twenty minutes for Scorpion Jack to thaw the crowd. Jake grabbed the microphone and announced some really fast numbers. The band went into a heavy metal routine. The music beat out loud and fast. Tune followed tune. Dance followed dance. The dancers closed their eyes and opened their minds. Jake, Dave, Kev and Liam, the stranger from outside the school, were no longer class-mates, but idols from the world of rock 'n' roll. And at the end of the night Jake took the frame of an old guitar he had found dumped beside a dustbin earlier in the week – took it and, to the horror of Mr Murray and the other teachers present, hopped across the stage pumping the flat of the guitar off the floor to the cheers of the dancers.

It was ecstasy; sheer ecstasy! When it was all over Jake was covered in perspiration.

Backstage they could hear the crowd in the hall roar for more.

'Will we do an encore?'

'Yes, but let's do something really wild. Something we've never done before.'

'Not on your life. We might get expelled.'

'Never thought of that. Anyway, heavy metal's not our scene . . . too tiring. Better do some serious music in future.'

'Like what?'

'Like what's cultured.'

A valid point could be made against the heavy metal routine Scorpion Jack sometimes played. Kev's father was still worried by some of the clientele the band was attracting to its gigs lately. There was too much of the punk rock element. The heavy metal routine would have to go by the board.

'Let's call a meeting to discuss the problem. Maybe we should bring in some more of our own songs?'

'And have someone steal them and put them on record?'

'We'll discuss it all at the meetin'.'

'When?'

'Tomorrow night.'

They went back on stage for the encore. They did a four-number set. They started with fast rock, then slowed the tempo down and played a few dreamy numbers for the smoochers.

Soon as the gig finished a bombshell dropped. Mr Murray refused to pay. 'For your school . . . and you expect money?'

No wonder Mr Murray was a maths teacher: subtraction was his forte.

Worse still, there was a post-mortem over the apples, pears and monkey-nuts that went missing from the van. Ger Sloane wanted compensation. He expected Scorpion Jack to foot the bill. It was a no-win situation. They hadn't any other means of transporting the gear to gigs. They had no option but to pay up.

School gigs? Miserly maths teachers? Stolen fruit?

Not on your life!

Never again! The school could go to hell!

A few days after Scorpion Jack's 'charity' gig at Bray Community College, Sandy Black, Gavin and Hammer were relaxing at their digs in London. Sandy was reading one of the Belfast newspapers. He pointed out a heading to Gavin and Hammer.

SANDY ROW MAN BEFORE COURTS

'I know him. That's the fella I brought the bag with the bullets to when I was home last summer.'

'What did he do?'

'Got caught smugglin' arms on the Larne to Stranraer ferry.'

'What's his name?'

'Sammy Miller. I'm glad I'm away from Belfast. Don't think I'd ever wanna go back.'

6

John Hallsworth finally got in touch with Elaine.

'Juventus! You want me to go to Turin?'

'A week's trial, all expenses paid. They'll sign you straight away if they're impressed.'

'I'm sitting my Leaving Cert in June. I won't be finished until the end of June.'

'I'm sure Juventus can hold back until you're finished your exams. End of June should be all the same to them. Do you think there would be a problem with your parents giving consent?'

'Not really. They're football mad. I'll ask and let you know.'

Elaine brought up the subject that evening:

'Da, can I go to Italy?'

'Italy? We don't know anything about Italy.'

'As well as football, they say they'll fix me up with a part-time job modelling leisure wear.'

'What about your running?'

'There's a lot of money involved. And a good job.'

'You'd be happy there?'

'I think so.'

'Well, if your mother agrees you can give it a try.'

Elaine couldn't see any problem coming from her mother. She'd agree.

Come the end of June, Elaine was all set to give the Italian Ladies professional soccer scene a try-out. She was looking forward to the challenge. But first there was the difficult matter of her Leaving Cert. She was a bright kid, a year ahead in school; but an exam was an exam.

The Leaving Cert – a giant-sized headache. Italy – a heap of fun.

By Christmas London Albion's Youth side were lying in third position in the South-East Counties Youths Division. Arsenal were ahead of them by three points; Tottenham by one.

The FA Youth Cup was due to start for London Albion in early January. Due to some mix-up over the league fixtures Gavin and Hammer were allowed home for Christmas holidays a week earlier than was the norm. They came home on the week-end that St Joseph's, Hammer's old club, were playing in the Mars/FAI Under-17 Cup, and decided to go to the game. They made their own way from Greystones to Blackrock where the St Joseph's minibus picked them up and brought them the rest of the way to the game on the north side.

As usual St Joseph's were taking the fixture very seriously. There wasn't any messing in the minibus, except to ask Gavin and Hammer what it was like to play Youths football in England. And, of course, a few questions were thrown in about the big-name stars on London Albion's first team.

On arrival, St Joseph's had to go to a Community Centre to tog out, as there were no dressing-rooms available at Belcamp College where the pitch was. At the Centre the opposition was milling around the team manager. There were at least twenty-five of them, all pleading for a game: skinheads, boot-boys, punk-rockers, you name it. The poor manager was flummoxed. He looked as if his very life was being threatened. St Joseph's squeezed past the melee and into the visitors' dressing-room. When they came back out the crowd had disappeared. Those who hadn't been picked stood outside the main door waiting, with the corner-flags, nets, and sundry bull-terriers and alsatians on leads, waiting for a lorry to pick them up and bring them to the pitch a mile-and-a-half away. St Joseph's got into their minibus and waited for the lorry to arrive and lead the way.

The lorry arrived. The opposition came out of the Community Centre and climbed on to the back of the lorry, their supporters and dogs with them. The referee travelled separately. At least three of the opposition appeared to be in their twenties, and three had beer bellies. As the Mars/FAI Under-17 Cup was restricted to U-17s St Joseph's began to feel suspicious and a bit nervous. Then a young woman arrived with a pram and got some of the players to lift it up on the back of the lorry.

'Here's your baby,' she said to one of the players. 'If you think I'm mindin' it while you go off and have a ball playin' football you've another think comin' to you. Keep him well wrapped.'

She climbed down off the lorry, leaving child and pram behind, the player left 'holding the baby' so to speak. The cavalcade took off. Hammer thought there was going to be slaughter. Skinheads and punk-rockers, all mixed up with alsatians and bull-terriers! They got to the pitch. The supporters ran all over the field, fencing with corner-flags, then putting them in place in the corners of the pitch. They tossed the nets at one another like gladiators; then they quietened and fixed them to the goalposts and crossbars and pegged them out at the back. A few of them took turns giving the penalty areas a quick run-over with a marker. Then they all withdrew to the sidelines. The referee moved to the centre-circle, called the toss, the players took up positions, the referee blew his whistle and the match started.

Once the whistle sounded and the game kicked off, the crowd became transformed. Before the game they looked as dangerous a crowd of skinheads and punk-rockers as could be got anywhere in Dublin. But once the whistle was blown they became great sports. Not that they didn't cheer for their team, they did. As for their team on the pitch, they never once queried the referee's decision. They were like perfect gentlemen. But they could play hard – very hard! However, they weren't very fit, especially the three with the beer bellies. They were only capable of standing around and lofting huge punts down the length of the pitch. The three of them were deployed in the centre of the defence, one acting as a covering player behind the other two – a slight over-exaggeration of what the term 'stopper' was intended to imply. They were definitely a lot older than anyone on the St Joseph's team.

All was scoreless until well into the second half. Then the baby in the pram began to cry, and its father was called off the pitch to quieten it. He was gone for quite a few minutes. The manager wanted to substitute him, but the player wouldn't allow it. St Joseph's scored a goal.

The opposition manager was disgusted.

'Get back on the pitch!'

'I haven't finished with the baby.'

'Get back on the pitch!'

The player got back on. Within five minutes the opposition equalized. The game went into extra time. The three with the beer bellies weren't too short of having heart attacks. It was sheer hell trying to hang on. St Joseph's were all over them, full of running but unable to score. Then with a minute of extra time left, as the ball was being cleared off the goal-line, it struck one of the beer bellies head-on and bounced into his own net. Hammer's old team won 1-2.

Gavin and Hammer thought St Joseph's had won the battle but not the war. They expected trouble. But the opposition couldn't have been nicer in defeat.

'Great game!'

'Great stuff!'

Skinheads, punks, beer bellies, and the father of the baby all offered their congratulations, and climbed back on the lorry for the return journey to the Community Centre.

The last Gavin and Hammer heard when leaving the

pitch was, 'Anybody got a nappy? The baby is after wettin' himself.'

Such were the trials and tribulations of U-17 football. Whatever about the weather, life was never dull on the playing fields of Dublin.

While he was home Gavin never got to see his ex-team, Cambridge Boys, play. The Christmas break was on. All schoolboy Leagues were closed down, friendlies included. But Gavin and Hammer got in some training with Lar Holmes's U-12 team and passed on a few tips. Two special training sessions were arranged. Full house. The U-12s were all ears. They were on their best behaviour for Gavin and Hammer. The Rivermount (Woodbine) duo even gave up smoking while they were around. But the one player who impressed Gavin and Hammer most was the Lollipop Kid. He had huge potential.

Lar Holmes was eager to talk to Gavin.

'I'm getting some hassle,' he opened.

'How come?' asked Gavin.

'That Glynn . . . the Riverside manager. He's been out here tryin' to sign the Kid. I've seen him and his car hangin' around Greystones after school hours. He'd better lay off, or I'll report him to the League.'

'Are you sure? Maybe he's out here for some other reason.'

'He's not! He's tryin' to poach the Kid!'

'There's no point in reportin' him if you can't prove it.'

'Prove it! He asked the Kid to sign. That's proof enough. That's the only proof I need.'

'Is the Kid stayin'?'

'Course he is. He's happy here. Anyway, his mother wouldn't let him travel in to Bray. If that Glynn doesn't lay off I'll have him done. I'll have him up before the League.'

'Lar . . . I hope you're not shoutin' at the players?'

'Course I'm not. I'm keepin' me mouth shut. I'm not

givin' out to no one, except Glynn. I'll lay the law down to him the next time I see him. I'll give him a right roastin'. Comin' out here and tryin' to poach the Kid. And another thing, see my big centre-half? Glynn is goin' around tellin' all the teams in the League he's overage. That's pushin' his luck a little too far.'

'Is he overage?'

'Course he's not. But thanks to Glynn half the teams in the League think he is. We're not due to meet Riverside again until well into the New Year. They did us out here. Harry Hennessy, you know. A damned disgrace! If Glynn doesn't lay off I'll do him in Bray. Mark my word, Harry Hennessy, or no Harry Hennessy, I'll do him.'

'How's the team doin'?'

'Not bad. A bit above mid-table. The kids are keen. They want to do well. Good bunch of lads. Riverside's goin' well. There'd be nothin' better than beatin' em in Bray and costin' em the League. That'd make my day. Glynn's bankin' on me losin' the head and shoutin' at the kids. Thinks maybe the team will break up then . . . But he's got another think comin'. The more I think of it . . . God, I think I'll pull one over him in Bray.'

'Lar, you want to watch you don't get yourself into trouble with the League.'

'Trouble? I don't know the meanin' of the word. Just Riverside better lay off tryin' to poach the Kid, that's all.'

It was obvious nothing much had changed since Gavin and Hammer's time with Shamrock Boys. The eternal hate triangle between Mr Glynn, Harry Hennessy and Lar Holmes was still in place.

Except for the two training sessions at the Railway Field Gavin and Hammer didn't see much of Elaine over Christmas, although they did make arrangements to go for a Christmas morning run over Bray Head. They were delighted to hear she had been offered a trial with

Juventus during the summer. Greystones was agog with the news. There was even talk of an Irish international cap in the not too distant future. So far only one international had come out of Greystones – Susan Hayden, a goalkeeper. Pity the Ladies Leinster League was closed down for the winter. Since the news of her prospective trial with Juventus broke a lot of people around Greystones would have liked to have gone to Cornelscourt to see her play.

The League wasn't due to open up again until mid-April. That wouldn't make it any easier for Elaine to keep her match fitness. But she was still going for cross-country runs over Bray Head and playing hockey for her school. The Leinster Schools Senior Hockey Cup was due to begin in January or February. Then the soccer season would start up again in mid-April. She'd have no problem with her fitness when the time came at the end of June for her trip to Turin. The trial was something to look forward to. Hopefully it would ease the tension over the build up to the Leaving Cert.

Gavin, Hammer and Luke went into Dublin to hear Scorpion Jack play three days before Christmas Eve. Venue – upstairs over a pub on Burgh Quay. The clientele – mainly weirdo-types and punk-rockers. Luke looked around to see if his two female punk-rocker 'associates' from the time at the Green Door were there. He didn't have far to look. They were sitting at a table pressed right up against the edge of the stage. They had the rest of their gang in tow. They always travelled in numbers to city gigs. They had no transport problems for Dublin gigs, as they only lived around the corner from Burgh Quay.

Kev's father shuddered in horror when he saw them. He consulted one of the bouncers.

'There'll be no trouble, mate, no trouble. See that little girl there? Tha's my little Maria.'

'Little Maria?'

'Yeah, me baby daughter Maria. She's a lady. You're not complainin' mate, are you?'

'Not really.'

'Ye wouldn't want to. See that girl sittin' beside Maria?'

'The chubby one?'

'Yeah, the well-built one. Well, she's Maria's best friend. They go everywhere together. You wouldn't want to complain 'bout her either. 'Because she's the boss's daughter. And the boss don't like anyone complainin' 'bout his daughter. He wouldn't let your band gig here any more. Anyway, there's no reason to complain, is there?'

'No,' gulped Kev's father. 'No reason.'

When Scorpion Jack came on stage they couldn't help but notice Maria and her friends. Maria kept on smiling and winking at Jake. During the break he even had to share a drink with her. Then afterwards she asked him for a date.

Panic stations!

'I'm married,' he lied.

'You're wha'?'

'I'm married, with two kids.'

In two shakes Jake could see Maria was beginning to seethe with temper.

'I seen you all over Dublin. I even went out to Bray. And all you did was lead me on . . .'

'I did not!'

'You did! Your songs was always for me.'

'What?'

'Aw, shut up! You oughta be ashamed of yourself. At your age. Married with two kids. I suppose you're signin' the dole as well?'

With that Maria gave Jake a knee in the groin. 'Love hurts,' she fumed. 'More for you than me.' Having said this she draped her leather jacket over her shoulders and led her cohorts down the narrow staircase to the street. They wouldn't be following Scorpion Jack any more.

Luke came across Elaine by chance getting off the Bray bus on Christmas Eve. She was laden down with Christmas shopping. He told her about Jake's fall out with Maria.

'It's a mighty dangerous life being a pop-star,' she laughed. 'Guess who I met in Bray?'

'Santa Claus, by the looks of things.'

'No, my ex-coach. She wants me to go back to athletics after Easter.'

'She's got some nerve. And you all set to go to Juventus.'

'She didn't know.'

'She knows now, doesn't she?'

'She sure does. They're having all these stars at the club: Catherina McKiernan and Sonia O'Sullivan. I won't be going.'

'I wouldn't mind meetin' Sonia O'Sullivan and Catherina McKiernan.'

'You could bring your pigeons along. Sonia O'Sullivan could give a few tips on how to race them.'

'You serious?'

'Of course not . . . Though one thing does worry me. People are expecting a lot to come out of this trip to Juventus.'

'Maybe they are. It's the talk of Greystones. It doesn't make it any easier for you, Elaine, does it?'

'It certainly doesn't. It's only a trial, initially. In a way, I wish nobody knew about it. Then, if I flunked it I wouldn't feel so bad . . . How's the pigeon world?'

'Rough. You can't go into a shop to buy some pigeon grub without other fanciers chasin' after you to find out what you're feedin' your pigeons on. Imagine what it would be like if you won one of the big pigeon-races. You couldn't pee but they'd be watchin'.'

'It's not that serious, is it?'

'Yeah, and worse. Most fanciers think more of their pigeons than their wives.'

'They mustn't believe in divorce, then?'

'Maybe they would, if they could spell the word.'

'Happy Christmas, Luke.'

'Happy Christmas, Elaine.'

On the way home, he thought how easy it was to talk to Elaine. Maybe he should get out more, get to meet more girls. Then he thought of her giggling class-mates. Maybe he'd better stick to pigeons.

For Luke, Christmas meant having his pigeons in top breeding condition. Already he had cleared his loft of all surplus birds and had got in touch by phone with Arthur Irvine (the pigeon breeder from Portadown who was largely responsible for setting Luke on the road to success in the pigeon-racing world). He wanted some advice. He felt he needed to introduce some new blood into his breeding strain. Arthur would be the man to put him right.

As usual, Mr Irvine came up trumps. He knew a fancier in the Bray area with whom he had a lot of pigeon dealings over the years. The fancier was now an old man who felt he could no longer cope. He had no choice but to get out of the fancy. Arthur Irvine reckoned Luke would add considerably to his breeding strain if he could persuade the old man to hand over his best stock birds. His name was Jack Brown.

'What's his address?'

'Hang on. I'll look it up.'

Luke held on.

Mr Irvine came back and read out the address. It was on the Boghall Road.

He then told Luke of an upcoming pigeon auction in Dublin.

'I'll be down. See you there.'

'Where's the auction?'

'The Sarsfield Club, Ballyfermot.'

'When?'

'Tenth of January.'

'Arthur, when you're comin' could you bring me a wicker pigeon-basket? They're too dear to buy down here.'

'For how many birds?'

'Fifteen. I'll pay you at the auction."

Luke replaced the phone and went out to the pigeon-loft to check the stock-book and decide how many new birds he would need. He'd have to go into Bray in advance and see the old man Arthur Irvine had recommended. He didn't want too many birds. There was no point in overloading the loft. Just a few would do.

The Sunday before the pigeon auction was to take place Luke got the bus into Bray to see what pigeons Jack Brown would let him have. He had already been to see him and it was clearly obvious that the poor old soul's pigeon-keeping days were over. Tragically, he had fallen out with everyone, especially those connected with the racing scene. Lots of local pigeon fanciers were interested in taking birds off his hands but he didn't want anyone to have them. In Luke's case he relented and said he could have the pick of the loft. He was a peculiar old man. But sometimes that was what old age did to people.

Jake went into Bray with Luke on the 84 bus to give a hand with the pigeon-baskets. At first the bus driver wouldn't let them on because of the baskets being too bulky. But he had a change of heart when he recognized Jake. He was well used to Jake hauling a guitar case on to the bus over the last few years. A few pigeon-baskets weren't any bulkier. Anyway, the bus wasn't overcrowded. There was plenty of room.

Jake was wearing a leather jacket with a technicolour scorpion emblazoned across the back. 'Scorpion Jack' was embroidered over it in gold.

'Advertising your band?' asked the bus driver.

'Yeah. If your bus is one big packet of Smarties, I don't see why I can't advertise a rock group.'

'How's the band doin'?'

'Like Dublin Bus. Behind schedule.'

'You'll pick up soon.'

'Yeah, when Dublin Bus takes to the skies.'

'You're havin' me on. Word is the band's pretty good.'

'Good to see the PR is workin'.'

On the journey into Bray Luke told Jake more about the old man they were going to visit.

'He told me to bring two barrels. That I'd get them dumped at the back of the factories on the Boghall Road.'

'What's he want barrels for?'

'Beats me. But he told me to bring two to his house when we collect the pigeons. I came into Bray yesterday and sure enough there was loads of barrels thrown out at the back of the factories. I threw two in a ditch. We'll collect them on the way to the old man's house.'

'How are we goin' to manage? We've already got the pigeon-baskets to carry.'

'He only lives up the road from the factories. Anyway, where I left the baskets is only a few hundred yards from his house.'

Luckily the barrels were still where Luke had left them. Jake pulled them by the rim out of the ditch.

The old man was waiting. He hadn't much to say. Not until they went into the loft. He told Jake to place the two barrels in the middle of the floor; Luke was to open the pigeon-baskets. He intended to give them twelve birds – his best stock birds.

'What are you going to do with the rest?' asked Jake.

'They're goin' into the barrels.'

Jake didn't understand what the old man meant by 'They're goin' into the barrels,' but Luke, being a pigeon-fancier, knew only too well. The old man intended wringing the birds' necks and tossing the bodies into the barrels.

Jack Brown picked up a pigeon and moved his hands through its feathers, slowly contemplating.

'What are you doing that for?' asked Luke.

'Touch is the best way to judge a bird's fitness. A smooth, silky touch and it's in condition; lumpy and it's not. I'm touching it for muscle. Smoothness is for muscle; lumpiness is fat. When you race a bird, two days before the race judge the bird by touch. If it's lumpy don't send it. Birds don't race on fat, they race on muscle. Ever hear that before?'

'No.'

Next thing, Jack Brown moved his hands to the pigeon's head. He gave a quick jerking twist and tossed the pigeon into one of the barrels. Jake felt that he was getting sick. He could hardly believe his eyes.

'See what he did?'

'Pigeon men do that all the time with surplus birds.'

'He killed the pigeon!'

'Didn't feel a thing, son.'

'Are you goin' to do the same with the rest?'

'Sure, all except the best. They'll go in your baskets. They ain't no use to me. I can't look after them. An' I ain't givin' anyone else the pleasure of ownin' them. People around here don't do nothin' for me. So why should I give'm me pigeons?'

'Luke, why don't you take them? It isn't right to wring their necks.'

'He's a pigeon man, son. He only wants the best and I'm givin' him the best.'

Jake felt disgusted.

Jack Brown began to feel through a second pigeon's feathers. Jake couldn't take any more. He bolted from the loft and waited outside.

Half an hour later Luke came out, his two pigeon-baskets full.

'You knew what those barrels were for, didn't you?'

'No, honest. I only knew when he said he was goin' to put the pigeons in the barrels. I couldn't take all those pigeons. I haven't room. They'd cost a fortune to feed.'

'You could have given them to some kids.'

'Well, if it's that easy, why didn't you take them?'

Jake hardly spoke on the bus-ride back to Greystones. Once or twice Luke tried to smooth over the situation but Jake was in no humour for excuses. He barely said good-bye to Luke when they got off the bus at Blacklion.

'What about the pigeon-baskets?'

'Carry them yourself.'

Although Jake was a joker, underneath he was very sensitive, especially when it came to animals being mistreated. He wouldn't walk up the road with Luke. He went off in the opposite direction.

'It's not my fault if the oul' lad wrung the pigeons' necks,' Luke shouted after him. 'It's not my fault. I didn't do it.'

But Jake wasn't listening. Luke picked up the pigeon-baskets and laboured across Blacklion in the direction of Kindlestown Park.

Hopefully, Jake would cool down in a few days and they would be on speaking terms again. He'd never had a row with Jake before. It wasn't as if either of them were to blame. If anything, it was the fault of the old man. He could have at least waited until they had left the loft before he wrung the pigeons' necks. That way Jake wouldn't have known what was going to happen.

Give it a few days and Jake would be as right as rain. He'd be up to the house, joking and trick-acting. If not, Luke would go looking for him and patch up the situation.

Two days later Luke called around to Jake and they made up. But Jake cooled considerably towards the pigeon-racing scene. He just didn't want to know. He had seen enough.

Luke went to the pigeon auction in Ballyfermot on his own. The journey entailed a change of bus in Dublin; Ballyfermot was a difficult place to get to from the south side. Only that he wanted to meet Arthur Irvine and collect the pigeon-basket he wouldn't have bothered. He wasn't over-fond of pigeon auctions. Usually the people who attended them were divided into cliques who had no time for young up-and-coming fanciers. But he hadn't met Arthur face to face for a long time and the auction gave him the opportunity. Arthur had come down from Portadown with a few friends. He had the wicker pigeon-basket for Luke, plus a few *Pigeon Gazettes*.

'I'm thinking of going for the big one, Arthur.'

'The King's Cup?'

'I've got the right bird. One bred off your hen. It's getting stronger all the time. It's the best flier I've got. It's an unknown. I'm goin' to spring it in the King's Cup.'

'Know what you do with a King's Cup winner, Luke?'

'No, what?'

'Put it to stud. That way you'll make money. Fanciers go mad for a youngster bred off a King's Cup winner. When do you intend to start training the bird for the race?'

'April should be time enough.'

'You want to go a little sooner. Listen out for weather forecasts, though. Good spring days you can't go wrong. Grubbing and vitamins are important, too. Another thing, same as all continental races, King's Cup birds are always released at first light. That's a factor a lot of fanciers don't allow for. Lots of pigeons are stunned by the lack of light on an early morning release. They don't get away. They're dazed. They either circle for too long or roost on something nearby. You'll have to bring your bird out for weeks in advance of the King's Cup and release it at the crack of dawn. You don't bring it out on its own, neither. You want twenty or thirty other birds being released with it. Make it feel cramped, just like the liberation from the transporter would be. It isn't easy training a King's Cup winner, Luke. It takes a lot of know-how.'

And Luke knew Mr Irvine had the know-how. He had three King's Cup wins to his credit. Mr Irvine was a top dog. Most Irish pigeon-fanciers held him in awe, and he was the centre of attention during the auction. There weren't many quality birds on offer. Mostly washed out Busschaerts and a few measly Krauths. Whoever had put them up for auction was certainly chancing an arm or two. Luke felt sorry for Mr Irvine and his friends travelling all the way from Portadown to look at such sub-standard rubbish. But Mr Irvine and company weren't totally wasting their time. They clinched a few nice deals outside in the car-park. Money changed hands. Most of it went into Arthur's pocket.

After the auction Mr Irvine gave Luke a lift into the centre of the city.

'They should have those auctions more often. Gives a man a chance of making some big-money Irish Punt deals for a change.'

He shook Luke's hand and watched him cross the road towards Butt Bridge and Tara Street Dart Station. 'Never trust pigeon-men,' he shouted good-naturedly after Luke. 'They're too crafty.'

Luke turned to reply, but the car was already turning into Gardiner Street, heading for the road north. Whatever about being crafty, one thing was certain: Arthur Irvine was a gentleman.

7

Almost immediately after the Christmas break London Albion drew Burnley in their first game of the FA Youth Cup.

Stevie Hodgson had the Youths totally hyped for the first leg at Burnley's Turf Moor. Bill Thornbull put them through sheer hell in the weeks leading up to the cup-tie. They hardly got to see a ball. It was all run, run, run, and weights in the gym. Hammer found the going particularly tough. He had been thrown in at the deep end as far as training was concerned. He asked Bill Thornbull to ease up on him during training, to let him adapt at a slightly slower pace.

'Full-time trainin' gettin' to you, son? You'll have nightmares over Highfield before I'm through with you.'

Instead of easing up, Bill pushed Hammer harder. He got aches and pains in places where he thought a person could never ache. But gradually he eased into full fitness and the pain and tiredness subsided.

The match against Burnley had London Albion under pressure. The Albinos' keeper brought off three great saves. Sandy took a shot off the line. Gradually Glenn Thomas and Hammer got to grips with the rangy Burnley strikers. Mick Bates came more into the game, and Gavin and Cyril Stevens began to get a little more of the ball. But there was no one to lay the ball off to; the support wasn't getting forward quickly enough from the midfield.

'Get forward. Don't just stand there. Get forward and support the man with the ball.'

After thirty-eight minutes Mick Bates played a ball to Gavin. Gavin moved forward, slowed down and shielded the ball, waiting for someone to come in support. He spotted John Palmer moving wide. He played the ball to him, ran into space for the return, beat one defender, then a second, and slipped the ball past the goalkeeper for London Albion's opening goal.

London Albion's second goal was a real peach. Gavin took hold of the ball on the edge of the centre-circle, swerved one way, then another, sending the defence into a knot. He let fly from the edge of the penalty area. The goalkeeper hardly saw the ball. It was a real pile-driver of a shot.

Burnley were beginning to lose heart. Some fellow with a Burnley cap and scarf got in off the terracing and began to pace up and down the sideline.

'Come on, Burnley, Come on, the lads. Real Madrid last week – Barcelona next week in the European Cup Final. Come on, the lads. Boring, boring Albion.'

'Who's he?'

'Some nut that comes to all the matches.'

'What's he doin' on the sideline?'

'Thinks he owns the club. Thinks he's Ralph Coates.'

'Who's Ralph Coates?'

'A baldy lad who used to play for Burnley years ago. He got transferred to Spurs.'

'Come on, Burnley. Give us the good old days.'

'Get off the line.'

'Now ref, don't start.'

'Take that man off the line.'

The one policeman on duty escorted the reincarnation of Ralph Coates back to the terracing.

Burnley pulled a goal back. Gavin smashed in a third goal. Won 1-3.

In the return leg, at Brompton, Gavin scored two goals for a 5-2 aggregate victory.

The 'nutter' from Burnley showed up at Brompton. He arrived at the Burnley dressing-room door during the half-time break for a cup of tea with another 'nutter' reincarnated from Burnley's past, Andy Lockhead.

In the next round of the Youth Cup, London Albion beat Liverpool 1-0 over two legs. They were two real tough matches.

The game at Anfield was a classic – one of the best games seen for years in the FA Youth Cup. Mick Bates scored the winner with a rasper from thirty yards into the Kop end goal. At the after match get-together in the players' bar a lot of envious eyes were on Gavin, Hammer, Cyril Stevens and Mick Bates. You could see that the 'Red Machine' fancied them. There was a lot of whispered talk about Cyril Stevens. Seemingly he had originally come from Liverpool, a Scouser, only too familiar with the environs of Goodison, Anfield and Stanley Park in between.

'You got a good team there. A good footballin' team.'

'Thanks,' gloated Stevie Hodgson. 'Think I'll have a Scotch and red. Better luck next year, lads.'

'Luck? Luck's got nothin' to do with it. It's the players. You got the players. Damned fine Youth team.'

Back down in London word was going the rounds in the world of London Albion that the Youth team were on a roll.

'Have you seen the Youth team?'

'No.'

'Go and see them. Great team this year.'

'Who're they playin' in the next round of the Cup?'

'Newcastle United at home in the first leg.'

'They played them last year.'

'Yeah, Newcastle beat them in the semi-final. This is the rematch. London Albion will stuff 'em.'

'What with, Mars Bars?'

'Yeah, Mars Bars. Just like wha' Paul Gascoigne used to do.'

'Where's he now?'

'Playin' on Mars, I think.'

Although there was a great sense of anticipation surrounding the Youths, the season wasn't going so well for the first team. They were losing matches. After a good start to the season, they slipped into the bottom half of the League table. John Warner wasn't exactly ecstatic with their results. The pressure began to get to him.

One evening Stevie brought some of the Youth squad to see Albion play away to Crystal Palace at Selhurst Park. London Albion lost 2-1. Stevie got the Youths into the Directors' Lounge after the match. John Warner was there. He was down in the dumps.

'Wretched, wasn't it? I don't know what's gone wrong. See him over there?'

'Ted Brinsley?'

'Sure, the London Albion chairman. He's gunning for me. Ever since we started losin' he's got the knife out for me. There's all this crap in the papers: "Boardroom discontent." "Manager losing his grip." Someone's leakin' stories to the press. I think it's him, Ted Brinsley. If he comes over here I'll punch him one.'

'Easy on, John.'

'I'm not taking much more of this crap in the papers. If it gets any worse I'm gettin' out. One player . . . I need one player . . . and Ted Brinsley won't give me the money. What does he want, relegation from the Premiership? The crap in the papers is even gettin' to the wife and kids. I've enough of the boardroom plodders. I'll get out. It ain't worth the hassle.'

John Warner edged across the lounge, further and further out of the chairman's sight. He edged to the door. Said good-bye to the nearest London Albion player and was gone.

The pressure had got to John Warner.

John Warner wasn't the only person under pressure. On the far side of the Irish Sea Lar Holmes was coming under the same sort of strain. There was talk of cut-backs at work. If the cut-backs came off, last in would be first out. Lar's job was in danger. Another few months and he would probably be back on the dole queue. The worry caused him quite a few sleepless nights. But he bore up well. At least he didn't let his fears show when he was around Shamrock Boys. He had learned to keep his cool. It was good to have a football team to keep his mind occupied. And it was good to have that kid Elaine around the team. She was good for his nerves. As for Jake . . . he had come on a lot in the last few years. He was a good kid – one of the best – the salt of the earth.

Shamrock Boys had some mixed results after Christmas. They were well out of contention, as were most of the other teams in the section. The League had turned into a three-horse race: St. Kevin's, Riverside and Crumlin. But regardless of League placings. Shamrock Boys were enjoying their football. Everybody was quietly contented at the Railway Field.

It was the calm before the storm. It broke during a home league game against Mount Merrion. During the course of the game the Lollipop Kid bent forward with his head to bring the ball under control. An opposing player went for the same ball with his foot high. Smash! The two players were sent rolling to the ground. The Lollipop Kid came off worse. Three of his teeth were smashed and blood was gushing from his mouth. Lar and Jake did the best they could for him. Play was held up for ten minutes while they decided whether to bring him home or to hospital. In the end, Jake brought him home to his mother. The Kid never stopped crying.

His mother, looking at the ruined teeth, was furious. She'd have to bring him to the dentist on Monday to get them crowned.

Some of the Shamrock Boys committee had been at the

match. They turned on Lar as soon as the Kid was sent tumbling to the ground.

'We told you so! We told you the Kid shouldn't be playin' U-12 football . . . It'll ruin him! . . . He's too young . . . It'll only break him up . . .'

Lar ignored the taunts; he was too busy looking after the Kid.

The Kid never totally recovered. He was scarred. Fifty-fifty balls! He wanted to know nothing about fifty-fifty balls.

Lar took it hard. He felt it was all his fault. He should have never played the Kid U-12. He had ruined a good player. Getting beaten didn't worry Lar that much. But to see a good player go down the tubes . . .!

The Lollipop Kid incident wasn't the only misfortune that made Lar Holmes feel miserable that season. Crumlin put in a protest against Lar's ex-Éire Og centre-half on the grounds that he was overage. Lar got called into the Dublin Schoolboys offices where the protest was heard and told to bring in the centre-half's birth-certificate as proof. He had to sit in front of a three-man protest committee, show them the birth certificate, and then leave the room while the other club secretary was called in. Then the committee discussed the matter in private. It was a straightforward case. The player was underage; Lar Holmes had no case to answer. The Crumlin manager was outside waiting for his club secretary to come out. He didn't believe the verdict. He screeched after Lar Holmes, 'That lad's overage! He's a banger!'

'He's not! What makes you think that?'

'That Glynn fella that manages Riverside out in Bray told me so.'

'He did, did he?'

'Yeah, he did. I don't know how you get away with it. But I'll be waitin'. I'll get you next time.'

'You've nothin' to get. There's no overages on my team!'

'There'd better not! Cause next time you'll be got!'

Lar didn't feel too good. Glynn had set him up. He was trying to muck-rake Shamrock Boys. It had been going on ever since the season started. Ever since Lar came back into football. And it wasn't that Lar had done anything wrong. He had kept the peace, been on his best behaviour, looked after the kids. And now this . . .

Riverside! Shamrock Boys were due to play Riverside in Bray in a few weeks in a return League fixture. Three weeks, wasn't it? Three weeks' time. He'd pull the wool over Riverside's eyes and send them packing.

Daisy Dunne was a brilliant footballer, about three months overage for U-12. He hadn't played much football in the past year. There was no team for him. The best Shamrock Boys could do was sub him up for the U-15s. But Daisy didn't like being a sub. Either he'd start the game or he just couldn't be bothered playing. In a way it was a pity because Daisy wasn't just only a brilliant player – he was a match winner. Pity was, he wasn't known outside Greystones. If he had been there would have been a lot of clubs wanting to sign him. But as it was Daisy was quite happy to stay in retirement as far as football was concerned, and to go out ferreting and hunting with dogs. He was a real country boy with a tossing of red hair and two feet that could make the ball do the impossible.

Lar Holmes went looking for Daisy.

'Play against Riverside?'

'What age?'

'Under-12.'

'When's it on?'

'Saturday.'

'In Bray?'

'Yeah, St. Gerard's. Listen, I won't start you. You'll only go on if we're losin'. And late in the game at that.'

'To score a few goals?'

'That'd be about it.'

'Sure Riverside don't know me?'

'Course they don't. Bring your gear. You've got gear, haven't you?'

'What if they ask me my name?'

'Just use the name I give you.'

'What if they ask for my signature?'

'Don't worry, I'll have it all worked out.'

'Do you want me to play flat out?'

'No. Nothin' flashy. Do just enough to win.'

'See you Saturday.'

'See you.'

Lar Holmes walked down the road. He felt a lot happier now that he had seen Daisy. One thing was certain: regardless of Harry Hennessy, Riverside would get a beating on Saturday. Daisy Dunne would see to that. Serve them right. They'd know better than to mess with Lar Holmes in future.

On Saturday, Daisy came on for the last eight minutes. Riverside were winning 1-0. They weren't quite sure where Daisy came out of. He hadn't been in the dressing-rooms before the match. He didn't seem to be on the sideline during the game either. He appeared out of nowhere, so to speak. Riverside were coasting: 1-0 with eight minutes to go.

Then Daisy came on. One - two - three! He scored three lightning quick goals. Mr Glynn wasn't much short of having a seizure. Harry Hennessy was bamboozled.

With one minute left, Daisy walked off the pitch.

'Get his signature! I want his signature!' screeched Mr Glynn.

But Daisy was gone. He disappeared between a gap in a hedge, out on to the roadway. He picked his football bag up from behind the boulder where he had hidden his clothes. He didn't bother to change, not until he got a good half mile away from the pitch. Then he went up Bray Main

Street and hung about for Lar Holmes and the team to pick him up for the trip back to Greystones.

Three goals – maybe he had laid it on a bit thick. But he decided that the third goal was the insurance goal.

When Lar came up Main Street he was beaming. Daisy could see they had won. Riverside's league hopes were in tatters.

'Thanks, Daisy.'

'No problem. I'd do the same for anyone.'

As a point of interest, Daisy had another nickname: 'Have Boots – Will Travel.' His boots were for hire, and not always at a price.

St Kevin's, Whitehall, went on to win the League, with Crumlin runners-up. Riverside finished in third place, with Shamrock Boys fifth.

Somewhere along the line, Lar's job with the County Council came under threat. There was talk again of cutbacks. The Union was called in. A picket was formed. Lar became one of the picket's leading lights. He was in fighting mood. There was consternation. Lar was getting out of control. Even the shop-steward was finding it hard to restrain him. Management wanted him out; he was causing too much trouble. The Union secretary was called in. Lar was told to belt up, or his job would be on the line. He fumed, he sulked. He thought of going to Liverpool and joining forces with his cousin who worked at Lime Street Station for British Rail. Sadly, it looked as if Shamrock Boys were going to lose him. Except to stand on the Kop he would never get involved in football again. But at the last minute he backed down and the strike was settled. Lar went back to work and settled into a peaceful existence: at least until football started again.

As for Mr Glynn and Riverside Boys, his blue Opel came to a nasty end on the Loughlinstown dual-carriageway. It careered out of control. Luckily, it didn't hit anything. A tyre burst and the car spun along the embankment before grinding to a halt on a broken axle. There were thirteen in the car. Mr Glynn and twelve players.

'I wish we could do that again,' said one of the players as the Opel was towed away to the Gardai Station for examination.

'It'll never do that again,' sighed Mr Glynn. 'It's ban-jaxed.'

'Mr Glynn, it was a great car.'

'You'll never see its likes again.'

'And know what, Mr Glynn?'

'What?'

'You'll never see the likes of us again.'

'No, never.'

True words. True words. They gave one last loving look after the car as it faded on tow in the distance. To hell with the match! They walked over to the far side of the dual-carriageway and got the bus back to Bray.

Both legs of the FA Youth Cup against Newcastle were crackers. London Albion won the first leg at Brompton, 1-0.

Gavin scored the goal. London Albion took a short corner and Sandy Black sent the ball high into the Newcastle penalty area. Cyril Stevens got a touch to the ball but it was cleared by the Newcastle defence . . . only for Gavin to send in a looping shot from the edge of the area.

John Warner was watching from the main stand. He was impressed by Mick Bates and Gavin. The first team were still faring badly. They hadn't pulled out of their slump. The way they were playing he could have done with Mick and Gavin on the team. As John Warner sat in the stand he even thought of Darren Blyth. Darren would have come through on to the first team if he hadn't blown his top. The main problem with the first team was that the goals had dried up. Darren would have solved the problem adequately. He was due to have a talk with Ted Brinsley, the Albion chairman, after the Youths game. Ted was going to come up with the money to buy a goalscorer, £1.8m was due to change hands in a deal with Manchester City. Pity Darren Blyth couldn't control his temper. Pity Gavin Byrne was still a little too young and inexperienced to shove into first-team football. Still it was good to be able to extract the £1.8m from Ted Brinsley. The new player had better be able to pop the ball into the back of the net or John Warner's job would be on the line, as well as the jobs of some of his back-room staff.

John Warner went to see the second leg of the Youths Cup-tie against Newcastle. He had signed the new striker from Manchester City. Luckily he had brought his goalscoring touch with him. First-team results were picking up. The pressure was off, or would be off in another few weeks. John enjoyed the trip north to Newcastle. He had really taken a shine to Mick Bates and Gavin. Cyril Stevens and Hammer weren't bad either. And that Sandy Black – he was a real trier – a terrier. The lad had guts.

The Newcastle crowd remembered London Albion from the previous season's joust.

'Where is Darren Blyth . . .? . . .a . . . a . . . ah . . . ah.'

Gavin soon gave the Newcastle fans an answer. After only six minutes he met a cross at the far post and sent a glancing header into the back of the net.

The Newcastle fans weren't put off in the least. They roared their team on with their unique Geordie chants. They weren't the most passionate supporters in the country for nothing. 'Wor lads are best. Come on, wor lads, We make 'em. We bring 'em on. The Board sells 'em. Away th'lads.'

After twenty minutes it began to rain, making the surface slippy. The Magpies were hell-bent on an equalizer. Hammer slide tackled the Newcastle centre-forward on the edge of the Albion's penalty area. The centre-forward went straight to ground. Hammer looked towards the referee and grimaced, half expecting the referee to give a direct free kick. But thankfully the referee waved play on and John Palmer played the loose ball out of defence to Mick Bates. It was real end-to-end stuff. Newcastle attacked time after time; London Albion counter-attacked. The rain continued to teem down. The goal mouths turned into quagmires. Back passes were forgotten about.

'Wor lads. Wor team.'

The tackles were going in hard but fair.

After forty-three minutes a Newcastle player was fouled just outside the Albion penalty area. The referee awarded Newcastle a direct free kick. The ball was played into the box. Glenn Thomas attempted to clear it but it skewed off his foot and got stuck in the mud. There was something of a scramble and a Newcastle boot connected with the ball and forced it over the London Albion goal-line. The Albion players protested, but the referee was adamant – a goal.

The half-time whistle sounded. Newcastle came back out for the second half all fired-up. They ran London Albion ragged. Shots went in from all angles. But the Albion goalkeeper held firm. The Albion scouting system had triumphed once again. The Midlands scout had come up with a goalkeeping gem. Some of the saves had to be seen to be believed. Right through the long, torrid second half the goalkeeper kept Albion in the game. Eventually the siege was lifted and Mick Bates caught the Newcastle defence square with a pass which Gavin narrowly put wide. Then Glenn Thomas went close with a header from a corner. Late in the game Sandy Black lofted a high ball into the Newcastle box. The goalkeeper moved to the edge of the six-yard box and timed his jump but the greasy ball slipped from his hands and fell straight to Cyril Stevens. He gratefully sidefooted it into the unguarded net.

In the dying seconds Newcastle pulled a goal back. But

it was too late; London Albion went into the next round on a 3-2 aggregate.

The Newcastle fans went home discontented. 'They closed wor shipyards, closed wor coalmines, an' stole wor players. Come on, th' lads.'

London Albion met lowly opposition in Wigan Athletic in the next round. It should have been a cake-walk, but they only scraped through on a penalty shoot-out. They had their share of injuries over the two legs; Gavin and John Palmer being out injured for the first, while another three players were ruled out of the return leg in Wigan. Stevie Hodgson didn't blame injuries for their poor showing. He gave them hell. He put it down to complacency and big-headedness. He gave them a tough spell with Bill Thornbull at Highfield plus a timely reminder of who they were (apprentices) by busing them into Brompton for a spell of maintenance work and brushing the terraces.

They had slipped a little in the League too. They definitely weren't in contention for winning the title. That honour looked likely to rest between West Ham and Tottenham. London Albion had Spurs at home last match of the season. They intended to do West Ham a favour: to give Tottenham, their deadly arch-rivals, a beating and deprive them of the League pennant.

London Albion met Derby County, the surprise packet of the competition, in the quarter-final of the Youth Cup. They beat them 4-2 on aggregate. In the semi-final they met Aston Villa and beat them handily enough. Gavin met Mr Norman, the Aston Villa chief scout, after the match. He gave Gavin a warm handshake and wished him luck. In the other half of the draw Spurs got beaten by Manchester United in the semi-final. The final was to be played over two legs: at Brompton and Old Trafford. The players could hardly wait.

A week before the first leg of the FA Youth Cup semi-final was due to be played Gavin was selected on the FAI Youths to play Northern Ireland. The game was played at Dalymount Park. Poor Hammer missed out on being selected for the squad. He lost out to an English-born player of Irish parentage. But there was always next season, his last in Youths football. The English-born player would be overage for the panel then. It would leave Hammer with more than an even chance of being selected. Anyway he could always take solace in the fact that the great Irish centre-half Paul McGrath was never capped at any level for Ireland, not until he got into the full international squad. And he could have been capped by England, as he had been born there, but the English authorities were totally unaware of that fact. One call to Old Trafford during Paul McGrath's early days at Manchester United and 'the Black Pearl' could have been lost to the green of Ireland.

But all that belonged to history and speculation. Now it was the Republic of Ireland against Northern Ireland in a crunch European Youth Championship tie. Both sides needed a win. Any other result and Romania would go through to the finals in France.

Sandy Black was playing for the North.

The game was scrappy. The night was wet and miserable. There was only about one hundred and fifty spectators at the game. There were a few louts beneath the shed at the St. Peter's Road end. They spent the whole match shouting abuse at the Northern Ireland players. They were pathetic. The best they could do was throw oranges at the Northern players and call them names. The whole shambles was an embarrassment, and all Gavin could do after the match was offer Sandy an apology. Apologies were also offered to the visiting officials of the Northern Ireland team. What should have been a great sporting occasion was marred by a handful of louts who in all probability didn't even know where Ireland was on the map, much less give a damn about the welfare of the country – bar, maybe, the welfare that would be due to them at the Labour Exchange.

For the record, the game was a scoreless draw, as grim and as drab as the midwinter weather that veiled Dalymount Park. It would have driven a guide-dog to depression. Ireland 0 – Louts 6. Both Irelands were out of the European Championships.

The FA Youth Cup Final was a much more wholesome affair. There was a real carnival atmosphere about both games and, as the first team wasn't doing so well, it helped to generate a happy feeling for the future around the environs of Brompton. The first leg at Brompton brought out the club directors in force. The Mercedes and Lancias were conspicuous in the parking spaces marked for club personnel. Even the first-team coaching staff and players put in an appearance. Everybody connected with the club was there, sitting patiently in the stands waiting for the game to start.

Manchester United had a masterful team – one of their best ever. They expected to beat London Albion. A draw at Brompton, then take them apart at Old Trafford. United were Kings of the North, having gone through their League season unbeaten. All of their players were Youth internationals, and one, an outside-left, was already an established member of United's first team and a full Welsh Youth international.

'What about the Welsh kid?'

'See to it that he doesn't get the ball.'

'But what if he doesn't stay out wide? What if he operates in the midfield?'

'What if he does? We know who he is. Mick Bates'll mark him out of the game. Ever see anyone outplay Mick Bates?'

'No.'

'So don't worry. Big names mean nothin' to our Mick.'

And Stevie Hodgson's forecast was correct. Mick Bates blotted the Welsh wonder completely out of the game. It ended in a one-all draw, with Hammer scoring his first ever goal for London Albion. But still Manchester United felt secure. They had the home leg at Old Trafford to look forward to and all the Mick Bates in the world would be incapable of stemming the surging urgency of the 'Red Devils' in front of their own supporters.

They were to be proven wrong. They came unstuck and Albion gave them their one and only beating of the season in a 1-2 victory. Gavin and Mick Bates scored the Albions' goals and sent the Stretford End home in abject misery. It was a fitting ending to the Youths season. They had carved a niche for themselves in the record books. There was a lot of celebrating around Brompton. London Albion may not have won the South-East Counties Youth Division, but they had won the FA Youth Cup. Not only was the team feted, but Stevie Hodgson, Bill Thornbull and all the rest of the back-room staff were suitably congratulated. The season had ended on a high. And to add to the sense of achievement Gavin and Mick Bates were blooded in a reserve-team fixture against Reading. They played two more matches on the reserves and then the season was over.

Most of the Youths were in their last season at Youth level. John Warner had a few tough decisions to make: who to retain and who to let go. The Youths were called individually to his office. The big axe was out. Mick Bates and Cyril Stevens were the only players in their last season as Youths who were retained. Gavin's professional contract remained intact. Hammer, Sandy Black and the young goalkeeper from Nuneaton would have to wait until they turned eighteen to know whether they would be offered professional contracts or let go.

It was a bitter time to make decisions, especially after

winning the FA Youth Cup, but as most of the apprentices who were let go found out, football managers lived in the present and not in the past. The past meant nothing to them. 'Today's hero is tomorrow's bum.'

It brought home a sharp sense of reality to Gavin and Hammer as they travelled home to Greystones for the summer break. The misfortunes of others helped to keep their feet firmly on the ground. Football wasn't all about glory and winning cups. Maybe it created dreams – but it just as ruthlessly destroyed them. One only had to look at Glenn Thomas and all the other ex-Youth-team players whom London Albion now deemed surplus to requirements. For them the glory days, as likely as not, were over. That was the reality; the hard facts.

Professional football was a cruel, uncaring business.

Apart from that, Gavin and Hammer were due back in London in a few weeks to sit their O Levels. They weren't too worried about the results. Next year, it would be A Levels.

8

Sandy Black was only in Belfast two days before the police picked him up. He was walking over Queen's Bridge when an RUC Land Rover pulled in beside him. Two RUC officers got out and spreadeagled him against the parapet of the bridge.

'You Sandy Black?'

'Yes, what's goin' on?'

'Just a routine investigation.'

'What are ye searching me for then?'

'Just routine. You're to come to the station with us.'

'I've done nothin' I don't wanna go. You can't just lift me off the street.'

One of the RUC men grabbed Sandy from behind with an arm-lock. 'Come easy, son.' There wasn't much Sandy could do about it, except get into the Land Rover. His shoulder felt sore from where it had rubbed against the bullet-proof vest the officer was wearing. A crowd had gathered too. He only hoped nobody had recognized him. One thing was sure: nobody from the Sandy Row area was on the bridge, otherwise there would have been a riot.

The ride to the RUC station took about two minutes. Sandy was rushed into the heavily fortified building and brought to a small room where an on-duty officer kept him company.

'What's all this?' asked Sandy.

'You been in trouble with paramilitaries?'

'Course not. I keep to myself. I've been away all year in London. I only came home two days ago. And now this.'

'Take it easy. There's a few questions need answerin'. You're being held under suspicion.'

'Suspicion of what?'

'Suspicion of being a terrorist.'

'I'm from Sandy Row. I'm not IRA.'

'The IRA is not the only terrorist organization in Belfast.'

'Meaning what?'

'You're bein' held under suspicion of bein' a member of the UVF.'

The words sounded like something out of a nightmare to Sandy. Only the nightmare wasn't finished with. Two detectives came into the room, took him out into the courtyard of the barracks and put him in the back of an unmarked car. They drove out through the main gate into the heavy Belfast traffic. The car didn't stop until they got outside Belfast altogether. Castlereagh Interrogation Centre! The nightmare was only beginning.

The two detectives checked Sandy in. They brought him to a sound-proofed room, put him sitting at a table, and taped the interrogation. They asked Sandy general questions about his background. They backtracked and asked him the same questions with a few new ones thrown in. They were trying to catch him out.

'I wanna lawyer.'

'A lawyer?'

'D'y' know where this is?'

'Yeah, Castlereagh.'

'Another thing you should know is – we do what we like here. You'll get a lawyer when we say so.'

Another barrage of questions followed. It was only when the name Sammy Miller was mentioned that Sandy had any idea of how the detectives could implicate him with terrorist activity.

'D'you know a Sammy Miller?'

'Not really.'

'Have you ever been to his house?'

'No.'

'Well, what's this then?' The detective turned on the TV

that was on a small table in the corner. A video came on screen. It showed Sandy with a blue hold-all walking along the street where Sammy Miller lived. Worse, it showed Sandy going up to Sammy Miller's door, knocking on it and going into the house.

The officer played the video back and froze the frame on a profile of Sammy Miller's face as he answered Sandy's knock.

'Know who he is?'

'Sammy Miller.'

'Sammy Miller, convicted UVF terrorist. They lifted him off the Larne-Stranraer boat a few months back. He had a blue hold-all similar to the one you handed him in the video. The hold-all had a few knick-knacks in it, plus an automatic pistol. Boyo, you're in trouble. You can have your lawyer now. Have you anything to say?'

'No.'

Sammy was held at the interrogation centre for twenty-four hours. Someone informed his people. They got busy phoning politicians, community leaders and John Warner in London. Everything was done to help him. But the police wouldn't release him, not until they had preferred charges.

'This can't go to court. The boy is innocent. We can talk it out. Bring charges and it goes on record. It could ruin the boy's future. Let him go, he's innocent.'

The police wouldn't listen. He was charged the next day with being a member of the UVF and released on bail. He was due to go before the courts in July. He would miss the start of the football season. Maybe London Albion wouldn't want him as a result of what had happened. But John Warner and Stevie Hodgson stood by Sandy. Out of their own pockets they hired a top legal brain for the case. Someone with a complete understanding of the local scene in Belfast. Someone who would be able to stand up in court and explain that Sandy Black was an innocent victim of the Northern Ireland situation, who deserved the benefit of the doubt. Someone who could convince the court that Sandy Black had, quite innocently, handled the blue hold-all. It was a tall order. Maybe London Albion didn't want to get involved in such a time-bomb of a case. But, privately, John Warner and Stevie Hodgson did their best to keep Sandy Black out of Crumlin Road Jail.

The wait until July proved nerve-wracking for Sandy. He didn't think much about football. He didn't go outside the house. His parents felt like sending him away on a short break to some place where he wouldn't be known, but the terms of his bail prevented him from leaving Belfast. He had to sign on at the nearest RUC station before ten o'clock each night. An innocent victim of circumstance, he was a prisoner in his own country. Only then did he realize there were probably plenty more like him in Northern Ireland. At least he had people to fight his case. John Warner, Stevie Hodgson and the local community were standing by him. His predicament, although serious, would have been a lot worse if there was no one who believed in him.

He phoned Hammer in Greystones, told him to tell Gavin. Gavin was shocked. Said he'd come up North and visit. Sandy told him not to.

'Why not?'

'You wouldn't like it. There could be hassle.'

From what they'd heard Gavin and Hammer didn't hold out much hope for the upcoming case. They felt that the law wouldn't show any compassion. They'd send Sandy down.

It was rough times for Sandy Black.

John Hallsworth had the final arrangements in place for Elaine Clarke to fly out to Turin for her week's trial with Juventus. He rang Massimo Tardelli in Turin for verification and sent on the necessary flight tickets to

120

Elaine in Greystones. She was to be met at Turin Airport and brought next day to a Juventus training-camp.

The Ladies Football Association of Ireland wanted to utilize the situation to generate some publicity from Elaine's trial, but she preferred to have no mention made of it in the papers – not unless her trial proved successful and she was signed by Juventus. The publicity would have meant a lot to the LFAI as they never got much publicity in the papers. They were keeping their fingers crossed though. If Elaine was successful with her trial, and if she went on to play for Juventus, publicity would inevitably follow, and there would be an upsurge of interest in women's soccer in Ireland.

Elaine flew out from Dublin Airport at the end of June, the Monday after she finished her Leaving Cert examination. Gavin and Hammer went with her to the airport, as well as her mother and father. There were also good-luck messages for her from the Leinster Ladies League and the LFAI. Crusaders AC also sent a good-luck message, but it was possibly out of regret, as they stood to lose one of their best prospects.

Elaine had to fly to Rome first and from there get a connecting flight to Turin. Both flights were uneventful, except that she felt very excited. What with her Leaving Cert finished, her school-days over, and now this trip to Italy, she felt a real sense of freedom. The whole experience was just fantastic. When the flight got to Turin she was met outside Arrivals by Juventus officials. A photographer and reporter accompanied them.

'Benvenuta! Piacere di conoscera.'

'Speriamo che ti piace di stare qui.'

Elaine felt embarrassed by the media presence, light as it was. After all, she was only in Turin on trial. What if she failed to make the grade?

A Juventus jersey was produced. The photographer got Elaine to pose holding it.

'Ah! Bene . . . bene . . .' Everyone was beaming.

Someone produced a baggage trolley. Elaine's suitcase and hold-all were placed on it and they moved off to a quieter part of the reception area. The reporter took a few notes, jotted them down in meticulous Italian. Luckily his English was almost as meticulous.

From there they moved outside. A classy limousine pulled in, Elaine was ushered into the back and whisked off to a hotel for the night.

Training was due to start the next day at a special training-camp just outside Turin. Elaine hardly slept a wink all night.

Next day, one of the Juventus staff picked her up after breakfast and took her off to the training-camp. She was introduced to the players. They nodded their heads and smiled at her. Not one of them could speak English. She realized it wouldn't be easy to settle in. If she came through the trial period successfully she would have to learn Italian.

A ball was produced. The Italians' technique was very good. They had plenty of vision and the professionalism of their game was unbelievable. Elaine wasn't sure if she had the class to compete with them. But she knuckled down, conscious of the coaching staff watching her from the sideline. She knocked a few balls about. Did some good things, made a few slip-ups. But the slip-ups were mainly due to nerves and not knowing the players. She felt the going tough. But she knew she could adjust, given the chance.

And Elaine was given her chance. Each day practice matches were played, with the emphasis on touch-football and on ball skills. She even had to undergo a rigid medical examination. After the first night she didn't stay in the hotel, but moved to the training-camp with the rest of the girls. Basically it was another hotel, only more secluded, more away from the public gaze. The discipline and regimentation was strict – absolutely so. It was difficult to fall into the routine. It was so totally different from the past few months, which she had spent in a slog of strenuous study. It was physical as opposed to mental strain and actually helped her to unwind after the rigours of her Leaving Cert.

Possibly it sounded a little too easy, but at the end of the week Elaine was offered a contract. The hard part for her would be to live up to the standards the Juventus management and fans expected of her. Every week there would be a pressure situation. She would have to learn to cope with that pressure. And that, along with playing in the toughest and best women's soccer league in the world, was reason enough to warrant the big money she was being offered. She was given a £20,000 signing-on fee, £550 per week, free use of a car and a rent-free apartment. And, of course, whatever she would be offered on the side as a part-time model.

Elaine was astounded by the terms offered.

'Whats the matter?'

For a second she was disorientated. She didn't know what to say. She was stuck for words. Her mind was a muddle. Then, for want of something better to say, she blurted, 'I can't drive a car.'

'You'll learn . . . maybe some Italian too.'

Elaine was given two weeks' leave to go home and make arrangements for a permanent move to Italy. When she got back to Greystones the news of her signing for Juventus covered the sports pages. The Ladies Football Association were delighted with Elaine's good fortune. They now had the heroine who, hopefully, would generate much needed publicity for women's soccer in the national newspapers, as well as being a role model for up and coming girl footballers. On all sides there was a deep sense of satisfaction.

It wouldn't be long before Elaine would be standing under the Italian sky hearing chants of 'Juve! Juve! Juve!'

Scorpion Jack was a real live act, perpetual motion in action. Somewhere during their performances the lights dimmed and four spotlights circled their silver-spangled clothes. The tempo of the music would lower, become almost pulseless, until the stage lights would trickle back on again, the beat of the music increasing to a quicker tempo than before. Then, before the next number was over, the tempo would slacken and the lights would lower for a second time, leaving the four spotlights to criss-cross the darkened stage and finally settle on the four band members. One by one the spots would fade – leaving only Kev silhouetted. The music, too, faded with the lights, until only the hush of the crowd became evident.

Then Kev played a few chords slowly, holding the audience entranced, gradually picking up the tempo. Then the lights would trickle back until the whole stage was revealed, the bass guitar joining in with Kev; then the lead guitar and the drums coming in together. The band was back in full flow, thumping out the fast rock numbers to the swaying crowd below.

Ecstasy!

Summer in Belfast wasn't easy for Sandy Black. Because he was allowed bail most people thought he would be acquitted. That there really wasn't a tight enough case. All there was, really, was a video of him entering Sammy Miller's house with a hold-all. His defence would argue that nobody could prove what was in the bag, be it guns, bullets or a kilo of cheddar cheese. As for entering a person's house, that couldn't justifiably implicate him as belonging to the UVF.

Then there was his past record. His record was totally

clean. Poor Sandy, he had never been in trouble in his entire life. But, the nightmare still lived.

The kids around Sandy Row were treating him with hero-worship. Not merely because he was on London Albion's books but because of the allegations that he was a member of the UVF. Leave Sandy Row and go down past Donegall Square and the people were giving him dirty looks. He wished he could just walk away from it all, but there was nowhere to go.

Just before the beginning of July, two weeks before pre-season training was due to start at Highfield, London Albion sent Sandy a letter saying he was to stay in Belfast until his trial was over and that they would review his situation then. But the trial was only a few days away! As of that moment Sandy felt that they didn't want him any more because of the implications of what he was being charged with. Were his days with Albion over? That, to him, was a worse calamity than the court case he was facing. It was the end of the world and Belfast was his hell.

Jack Warner and Stevie Hodgson knew nothing about the letter London Albion had sent to Sandy Black. That is, not until they were called into Brompton for a meeting with the directors. The meeting was fixed for ten-thirty. 'Just the right time for Ted Brinsley and company, before heading off for a game of golf,' commented John Warner. 'I wonder what guff we'll have to put up with this time?'

John and Stevie gave a quick glance over at the spaces reserved for the club's directors in the car-park. All the spaces were occupied. Unusual! Something of paramount importance had to be afoot. Directors never appeared *en bloc* at Brompton unless the first team were in the hunt for a major trophy, or if there was a power struggle within the club. Not even the sacking of a manager could produce a full muster of directors.

But there was a full muster now. As John and Stevie

walked up the staircase towards the boardroom they tried to think over what had possibly gone wrong. The summons to the boardroom had them puzzled.

The directors, especially to the uninitiated, could be very intimidating in the cocoon of their plush, mahogany-panelled boardroom. In a way it was like facing a firing-squad, only this firing-squad wasn't carrying rifles; it was aiming cannon.

Ted Brinsley did all the talking. His huge frame dwarfed everyone else. Once he started expressing himself no one else could get a word in. He was always the dominant force in the boardroom.

'The boy in Belfast . . .'

'Sandy Black?'

'You had no right to get involved in hiring his defence.'

'Ted . . .'

'Your action could compromise London Albion.'

'What we do on a personal level is our own business.'

'You are missing the point. You are associating the club with a suspected terrorist. Nobody involved with this club can be seen to take sides in such a case. It is too controversial a matter. Under the circumstances you will have to withdraw your offer of legal aid.'

'The boy is innocent. He wasn't involved in anything subversive or devious. He took the hold-all in good faith.'

'That's not the way the public will view the evidence. And the public's perception counts. Withdraw your offer of legal aid. And we don't want that boy back at this club.'

'Even if he is proven innocent?'

'Quite definitely not! There is never smoke without fire. There are those who will always believe he is guilty. Under the circumstances we want him gone.'

'And you want the directive to come from me?'

'Yes. It's your job.'

'Give the lad a break.'

'It would be too damaging to the club. He has to go.'

John Warner knew there was no point in arguing further. The directors were holding a gun to his head. It was quite simply a case of giving Sandy Black the heave, or getting the sack. He masked his feelings, said no more, and listened as Ted Brinsley rambled on about not wanting the good name of London Albion embroiled in controversy over the Sandy Black affair.

Life at London Albion would go on as before. Sandy Black would have to make a new start for himself elsewhere. The parting of the ways had come. The future looked very bleak indeed for Sandy. What with the court case and London Albion cold-shouldering him, his aspirations seemed totally shattered.

When Sandy's case came to trial he had the same defence team that John Warner and Stevie Hodgson had arranged. The lawyers took the case on reduced fees and a special fund was set up in the Sandy Row to meet the costs. He was found not guilty and released immediately.

The case made headlines in the media. The fact that he was an ex-London Albion apprentice and that Albion had decided to kick him out was given due prominence in the reports. Most of the relevant details made the papers. It didn't make good reading from the Albion viewpoint.

As soon as the case was over John Warner got on the phone to Sandy.

'Sorry about what happened, Sandy.'

'It's not your fault.'

'Our hands were tied. What are you going to do football-wise?'

'I don't know. There's not much really. I might get fixed up with an Irish League team.'

'You'd be better off away, Sandy.'

'I know. But after the publicity of the court case nobody'll want me in England.'

'What about America, Sandy?'

'America?'

127

'Yes, America. I've a contact there. A fella I used to play league football with. He could get you in as a pro on the indoor soccer scene.'

'I don't know. America's a long way off.'

'You'd get no hassle. And it's not that far. Only a few hours' flying time. It'd be a good opening, give you a fresh start. And there would be a good sideline coachin' kids. You'd make a good living. And you'd get away.'

'Maybe you're right. There's nothin' else on anyway. Nothin' at the moment.'

'You'll go then?'

'Sure.'

'I'll ring you back in a few weeks with the details. Put in for a visa.'

'The court case wouldn't go against me, would it?'

'No. I'll sort all that out. That's one favour Albion can do for you. They owe you one. See you in a few weeks' time.'

Six weeks later Sandy Black flew out to Florida. Life was good to him in America, much better than it possibly could have been under the shadow of suspicion in Belfast.

One thing he knew: Belfast would never change.

9

While Sandy's world was crashing around his ears, Luke was preparing for the biggest event of his life, the premier race of the season, open to birds from all parts of Ireland – the King's Cup.

The King's Cup attracted the elite of racing pigeons, about three from each loft. They raced from Rennes in France, and there were fabulous prizes on offer for the winner, especially if the winning bird was heavily pooled. Luke had three birds entered.

The birds were due to be liberated in Rennes at approximately six o'clock on the Friday morning. The flying time from France to Ireland was between nine and ten hours if the weather was good and there was a strong following wind. In bad weather it could take anything up to twenty hours, even two or three days if the birds had to fly against a strong wind. Some birds would drop out along the way and rest, even forage for food, but the well-disciplined fliers would make a straight run for the home lofts.

Luke had to get his birds to the collection point in Bray on the Wednesday morning before the race. A club member had agreed to take all the Bray-entered King's Cup pigeons to Lisburn in Northern Ireland, so that the formalities, such as rubber-ringing the birds, could be completed. Lisburn was the control point for the race and all the competing birds, regardless of origin, had to set out from there. The birds were then put into a pigeon transporter which travelled to France by ferry and road.

The next day, Thursday, Luke had to bring his racing-clock to the Stillorgan Pigeon Club in County Dublin, so that it could be set against the Master Clock. There were other setting centres around Ireland, but the clocks all had to be set at the same time, and synchronized with the Master Clock in Lisburn.

Calculating race times involves highly complicated procedures. As the pigeons fly back to different lofts in various parts of the country, some will have a longer distance to fly than others. Even in the same town, or village, no two distances are equal. To balance out the obvious variation in distance between the starting-point of the race and the home lofts, pigeon-race organizers use different mathematical systems. Calculations are carried out to within 10 metres between the liberation point and the home loft, under a system known as co-ordinates. Another system of mathematical calculation is based on velocities.

More headaches. Yes! Pigeons are identified by a rubber ring with a number, attached under the observation of an official, and recorded. When the pigeon flies back to the home loft after a race, the ring is placed in a thimble and inserted on to the pinion set in a small aperture in the racing-clock. The time is recorded on a paper tape inside the clock, beside the thimble which holds the rubber ring – there is an inbuilt security system to prevent cheating. The mechanism ensures that a hole is punched at the start and end of the paper tape. Any illegal opening of the clock causes an additional hole to be punched on the tape, and as three into two won't go, three holes means the clock has been tampered with.

But enough about complications. Luke brought his clock to Stillorgan and had it set against the Master Clock. Intelligence report: three thousand pigeons had been entered for the King's Cup – all the top birds from their respective lofts. To win would be the achievement of a lifetime.

The pigeons, in the meantime, were on their way to

France where, at precisely six o'clock on Friday morning, they were released. The race was on!

Once the pigeons were released, the only rule that really mattered, was that an entrant had a limit of three hours after his first bird clocked into the loft to get to the centre where his clock was set. If he didn't get to the centre within three hours his first bird would be immediately disqualified.

Verification of who had won the race was usually known by the Friday night. All a fancier had to do was to ring the pigeon-line in Belfast and they could, within reason, give the name of the first pigeon home. Official confirmation usually followed in the form of a letter. But if the pigeon-line gave a name as a winner, that was it; the winner was known.

On Friday Luke was at the loft waiting from two-thirty onwards. He had heard the birds were released at six am on Friday. Weather conditions were near perfect and there was a following wind. The pigeons would be flying at approximately fifty miles per hour. To be in with a winning chance Luke calculated he would want his first bird back by three-thirty.

Deadline was approaching when Luke saw his first bird come in.

Hammer had come tearing down the road on a bicycle. The bird looked a pin-prick in the distance. Hammer was shouting out, 'It's comin'! It's comin'!'

The bird was flying low and strong. It swerved over the loft and dropped on to the sputnik, and in. Luke rushed into the loft and caught the bird firmly in his hands. He took the rubber ring from its leg, put it into the thimble and jammed it through the aperture in the clock.

The time registered three forty-eight pm.

Eighteen minutes outside his estimate. Would that be good enough?

'Where did you see the bird comin' from?' he asked Hammer.

'Just down the road.'

'Were there any other pigeons coming over?'

'No, just the one.'

'Do's a favour?'

'What?'

'Go back down, and watch if any more come over. I'll be down in a few minutes. I just want to feed the bird and make sure it's all right.'

Luke's second and third birds came in an hour later, within twenty minutes of one another. But the second and third bird were of no real importance; the first one was the one that mattered. Under the rules of the King's Cup he had three hours in which to register the time of his first bird.

By now Jake and Gavin had come along.

'Hear you got a bird back.'

'Three,' corrected Luke.

'Any sign of more coming over?'

'No.'

'Hammer's just seen a few headin' on towards Bray and Dublin.'

'Another twenty minutes and they'll be comin' in their droves.'

'What do you think of your chances?'

'Not bad. On time I'd have to be pretty close to the top.'

'Can we go to Stillorgan with you?'

'Of course.'

Luke's father was home by five o'clock. They got into the car and were off. The traffic was very heavy between Greystones and Bray, but once they got on to the dual-carriageway they were in Stillorgan in a matter of minutes.

There were others there already, clocking their birds in: fanciers who lived fairly close to Stillorgan. Luke had registered the fastest time of the lot.

A few more clocks came in. Still Luke was the fastest. It went past the deadline for Luke's time to be beaten; the three hours clocking-in rule had passed. He was the winner in the Dublin area, at least.

His finishing time had been telephoned through to Lisburn at seven-fifteen. Luke, Gavin, Hammer and Jake hung around the clubhouse until eight-thirty, then Jake had to go. He had a gig in Bray. He got a lift from someone who was going back that way.

At nine o'clock the Stillorgan club secretary rang the pigeon-line in Belfast and was told that Luke was the clear winner.

He had won the King's Cup!

There was pandemonium in the clubhouse. It was ten-thirty before they got out of the place. They dropped off at the rock club in Bray, Luke's father included, to tell Jake of the win.

He had won the premier award in Irish pigeon-racing! The strain of his winning bird would be worth big money. He had made it, thanks to Mr Irvine in Portadown who had given him the hen and the address in Belgium where he had picked up the cock from which the King's Cup winner was bred. Then there was all the advice Mr Irvine had given him along the way. He owed him everything.

Next day he sat down and wrote a letter of thanks. (Years later he found out that Mr Irvine had had a son the same age as Luke, who had been killed in an accident. The lad had been pigeon mad. Luke couldn't help but feel that if he had lived he would have won the King's Cup. Mr Irvine had given him the bird intended for his own son. For that he was eternally grateful, and not a little saddened.)

One of his prizes for winning the King's Cup was a car.

As Luke was writing the letter to Arthur Irvine two pigeon officials came to his door and Luke brought them out to his loft. They took the winning bird about a hundred yards down the road and released it. It flew up in a circle

133

and straight back into the loft, final proof that the bird was Luke's. All the rules had been complied with. Luke was confirmed as winner of the King's Cup.

Business had slumped for Kev's father. His factory was involved in turning out women's fashions for some of the big Irish department stores. He also had a line into the United Kingdom market. But that was a tricky exercise: attempting to balance the *punt* and the £ sterling, while at the same time trying to be competitive. There was a recession. At first, he tried to ignore the fact. Business would pick up. Everywhere was in a slump situation. Ireland . . . Britain . . . everywhere. It got to the point where he almost dreaded going to the factory. Opening the mail was a nightmare. Bills . . . bills . . . bills . . . Answering the phone was almost as bad. And while he was being pressed for money, his customers weren't settling their accounts in time. There was a real cash-flow problem. And relentlessly every week, week after week, there was a wage bill to be met.

He put all his efforts into trying to drum up business by going out on the road, calling to stores personally, offering discount prices. He racked his brains for ideas, gimmicks to zip up the cash-flow. It was all so time-consuming that he had to give up managing Scorpion Jack.

'Dad's not managing us anymore.'

'Had enough of us, has he?'

'No, it's the factory. Business has gone down. He wants to put more time in to get it back on the rails.'

'Good for him. We'll get along. Hope everythin' goes all right for your Da.'

'It will. It's only temporary. He'll give us a hand soon as the factory picks up again.'

Jake, Dave and Liam thought no more of Kev's father's problems. He drove a big car: a Mercedes. He was a wealthy man with a big house and regular holidays to the world's most exotic destinations. There was no shortage of money. Business would pick up. Just a few cut-backs in the meantime. The family wouldn't go hungry.

The lads got on with band rehearsals at the factory. They practised two evenings a week and sometimes on a Sunday afternoon. The rough edges were mostly smoothed out by now. They had become very competent. They still gigged at the Green Door in Bray. And they had moved up a few notches on the Dublin scene. They were taking the Baggot Inn by storm on Tuesday nights. What was more, there wasn't a punk-rocker in sight. Business was good. It could have been even better if they weren't still at school. They were strongly tempted to chuck school in but their parents wouldn't let them – that is, all except Liam, who took over negotiating gigs and running the business end of the band in his spare time. The money end was picking up too, though they still owed Kev's father the best part of the band equipment.

As for Jake and Dave, their creative output was maturing all the time. They had written quite a few extra songs; catchy numbers with a universal appeal, though some were anti-political, anti-social. But most of their songs were written with one intention – to sell well commercially. There were no flies on Jake or Dave when it came to knowing what the market wanted. Somewhere along the line they could all see a big future for Scorpion Jack. The indications were evident. They were drawing good crowds to their gigs; there seemed to be a buzz on stage when they performed; their confidence was rock-steady; everything was right, including their hunger to succeed.

Kev's father had to turn to the banks to keep the cash-flow from drying up. He had to borrow. Loan interest rates were high. Then the bank manager called him in – his overdraft was getting out of hand.

Around the end of June Scorpion Jack got a real shock. Kev rang them individually.

'My Da's in trouble. The factory's gone bust.'

'What d'a mean?'

'My Da's gone bankrupt. The bank's moved in and closed down the factory . . . Even worse. My Da owes tax. They've put the sheriff in.'

'The sheriff?'

'Yeah, he has special powers. He impounds everything on the premises and then they sell if off against the money that's owed.'

'You mean everything that's in the factory will be sold off?'

'Yeah, everything.'

'Our gear's in there. Guitars, amplifiers, drums, the lot. They can't take our gear. It doesn't belong to them.'

'They have a court order. Vans, merchandise, fittings, our gear, the lot! They can take everything. They moved in this afternoon. They told the staff to clear off and closed the place down. My Da's hopping mad about it all. He was in Dublin when it happened. When he came back the factory gate was locked and he couldn't get in because they'd changed the lock.'

'Did they get his car?'

'No. He had it with him in Dublin.'

'What are we goin' to do about our gear?'

'Don't know.'

'Maybe if we ask they'll give it back.'

'They won't.'

'Let's meet later and see what we can do. If we don't get our gear that's the end of the band.'

'There's nothing we can do.'

'There must be something.'

'There's nothing. It's the end.'

'See you later. We'll meet up at Tony's Cafe. Be there!'

'Right. But there's nothing we can do. The whole thing's finished.'

When Jake, Kev, Dave and Liam met up it was sad faces all

round. They sat at a table at the back of Tony's, where they sometimes met up when hanging around Bray. It was the same cafe where a few years previously Liam had inquired if they needed a drummer. They liked the place. Tony, the proprietor, didn't mind them sitting over a cup of coffee once they kept quiet. Tony was a soccer fan. He came from somewhere in South Italy and was a long-term fan of Cagliari from Sicily. He was always talking about the good old days and Luigi Riva, whoever he was.

'Who's Luigi Riva, Tony?' asked Jake.

'Luigi Riva was the best player ever to play for Cagliari. He was a master.'

'How come we never heard of him?'

'You are too young. Whatsa got you in here tonight?'

'Trouble. The sherriff's in town.'

Tony shrugged. The sheriff? He didn't get the connection.

He put four coffees and cream on the table and went back to tend to the fish 'n' chips customers at the counter.

Just looking across the table at Kev was doleful. It was easy to see he felt a sense of shame. His brothers and sisters probably felt the same way too. The factory closed up and his father declared a bankrupt! The lads could see that he had been crying. His eyes had that red, crying look about them. He looked absolutely devastated. He had got up that morning, one of the better-off kids in Bray. By afternoon his father's factory was closed down, his assets frozen and the whole family humiliated. Life had turned on its head in a matter of hours. There were even rumours that his Dad was going to leave Bray. That the whole family was going to up and leave before the tax man and bank regrouped for further demolition.

'Have they taken anything out of the factory yet?'

'No, it won't go for a few days. They'll have to make an inventory first.'

Jake was feeling militant. 'I suggest we go in there tonight and take what we can with us.'

'We can't do that. That'd be breaking and entering. It's against the law.'

'Who cares? I want my guitar! No half-baked sheriff's walkin' off with my guitar. We can climb over the factory gate. Kev, you've got keys to the doors.'

'They've changed all the locks.'

'We'll get in through a window then.'

'The place is alarmed.'

'That's just great . . . The control box! D'you know the code for the alarm?'

'By the time you'd turn it off every squad-car in Bray'd be down there. You'd be only wasting your time, Jake. Anyway breaking and entering is out. You can go to jail for that.'

'For recovering our own property?'

'That's the way the law works.'

'Now I know how Jesse James must have felt when the railroad company swindled him out of his farm. Know what we'll do?'

'No, what?'

'We'll go down tomorrow when the factory is open. Walk in and grab the stuff.'

Liam looked at Jake and shrugged. 'I'd look great takin' the drum-kit. What am I supposed to use, a fork-lift?'

'Just take what you can grab.'

'That'd be the drumsticks.'

'It wouldn't work. Just walkin' in and out with our stuff. We'd be stopped.'

'It's worth a try,' blazed Jake. 'I seen a sheriff take over a shop in Bray once. He went in with his men, threw the staff out. They put on white shop-coats and sold all the stuff off. We'll get a few white shop-coats. I know a girl who works in a pork butchers. She's mad about us. She'll get a loan of a few white shop-coats. We'll put them on and go into the factory.'

'They don't wear white shop-coats in factories.'

'Don't they? Anyway the coats'll make us look kind of official. It's worth a try.'

'Jake, you're daft.'

'Who's on to give it a try?'

There was no immediate response.

'I will,' Dave succumbed. He felt stupid. The idea was scatterbrained. It hadn't a chance of working. But he had to do something. He wasn't prepared to give up his guitar without a fight. Jake's plan was so daft it just might work.

'What about you?' Jake asked Liam.

'I don't know. Get me a white coat. I'll go down anyway. It's just that the drum-kit is so bulky. I'd probably get out with nothin'.'

'What about you, Kev?'

'Leave me out. My father's in enough trouble already without me putting my foot in it.'

Jake understood his predicament. They all understood. Kev had had enough. He was sick to the pits.

'Right,' said Jake. 'We'll meet at half-ten, up the road from the factory. I'll organise the shop-coats. Me and Dave will go in first. If it works, Liam, you can go in after us. Maybe we'll go back in too and give a hand with the drums. We'll play it by ear and see how it goes.'

'What if it doesn't work?'

'Just run for it.'

Half-ten next morning Jake, Dave and Liam met up. Jake and Dave put on the white coats and told Liam to stay put, not to go near the factory until they came back out. Liam didn't complain. He wasn't too keen on going into the factory anyway. Jake and Dave weren't gone long. They strolled in through the factory gate and then the main door. The sheriff's men were all there, sifting through the stock and getting it ready to be taken away. Not one was wearing a white coat.

The men were busy. But not too busy to glance at Jake and Dave and remark about the stupid white shop-coats they were wearing. Still, they weren't challenged, or asked what they were doing on the premises. They walked right through the factory to the storeroom where their band equipment was.

'How'll we get it out? We're sure to be stopped.'

'Put it out of the toilet window and collect it later.'

'It won't fit out the window. We'll have to think of somethin' else.'

They put on their thinking-caps.

'The roof-space.'

'What?'

'We can jam some of it between the roof-space and the ceiling. Leave it there and hope to move it later when we get a chance.'

'We'd need a ladder.'

'To hell! We'll just take the guitars and walk out.'

'What about Liam's drum-kit?'

'Not much we can do. It's too bulky. If we get out, let him come in and take what he can himself.'

Jake and Dave took their guitars. In addition Dave stuffed a microphone in his jacket pocket. Jake grabbed at one of the practice amplifiers but it was too bulky to manage. Instead he took Kev's guitar in his spare hand.

They left the storeroom. Went back out into the corridor. Turned right, then left. Then through a room with row upon row of ladies' fashion dresses. The sheriff's men were busy itemizing racks of clothes.

'What's up with the white coats? Painters moving in?'

'What's the idea of the guitars?'

'We're bringin' them to the Boss.'

They bumped into a few more of the sheriff's men, all too busy to pay much attention to them. Before they knew it they were at the main factory door. They took off the white coats and ran for their lives.

As soon as Liam saw the guitars he wanted to go into the factory for his drum-kit.

'It's too bulky.'

'I brought a pliers. I can take the kit apart, pack it into somethin' and walk out. Want to give me a hand?'

'Jake will.'

Jake and Liam went off towards the factory, while Dave brought the guitars to the Green Door on the Albert Walk. Jake had already made arrangements with 'Big Red' to store any equipment they might salvage from the factory, at the night-club. In fact it was 'odds on' that Scorpion Jack would be having their band rehearsals at the Green Door now that the factory was no longer available.

Two hours later Dave was still at the Green Door waiting for Jake and Liam to get back from the factory. He was worried. They should have been back long ago. They must have got caught trying to smuggle the drums out of the factory. Just as he was giving up all hope the two lads arrived at the Green Door, drums and all.

'What kept yous? I was beginnin' to think you had got caught.'

'We did,' sighed Liam. 'We'd got everything done. Disassembled the drums, packed them in boxes, and made for the door. But this nosy ol' lad stopped us and brought us into an office where the sherrif was.'

'If you got caught, what are you doin' with the drums, then?'

'It turned out that the sheriff is me uncle.' Liam exploded with laughter. 'He let us go. Look, he gave me this for me Ma.'

He unwrapped a brown paper parcel he was holding and shook out a full-length party dress in front of Dave.

'He gave you that for your Ma?'

'Yeah, he was goin' to give me a second one, only I said my Da doesn't wear dresses.'

The three lads laughed. Scorpion Jack were back in business.

10

A few days before pre-season training was due to begin at London Albion, Gavin and Hammer called around to Elaine's house. She had only returned from her trial with Juventus, and was due to move permanently in a few weeks' time.

She was in great form. They decided to go into Greystones. Maybe have a cup of coffee. Maybe pay one last summer visit to the Railway Field.

They drifted down to the harbour first and sat in the lee of the grey-slabbed pier wall. Kids were going in and out of the Anchor Amusement Arcade opposite. There were a few pensioners on the North Beach. It was only early yet. Another hour and the harbour area would be jammed.

Then Jake and Hammer came on the scene.

A few small kids were out on the rocks behind the pier, rooting in crevices. The sun was getting pleasantly hot. Voices carried lilt-like across the looseness of the broken harbour wall.

'Remember me . . .?'

A tall scraggy youth had ventured on to the pier. 'Remember me?' he repeated. 'I used to play football with you for Shamrock Boys.'

'You're Robert Smyth, aren't you?'

'Yes. Mind if I join you?'

'Course not.'

'You're all doing very well for yourselves.'

'Kinda.'

'Nothing much has changed around here, has it?'

'Suppose not.'

142

'Greystones is one of those places that will never change.'

Jake nudged Hammer. Robert Smyth wouldn't change either. He was still as posh as ever. Though what he said about Greystones was true. Nothing much ever changed, or would change, in Greystones. The sea was still alive, the boats permanently beached on the stony shore which formed the lip of the harbour. And the night-time fishermen on the South Beach would for ever stand, custodian-like, beside feeble lantern-lights and the iron rests which supported the fishing rods whose lines of cat-gut hung taut and invisible in the darkness.

Robert Smyth was speaking again. 'I've just finished the Leaving. I hope to go to Trinity . . . Play some rugby . . .'

Bully for him.

'Like to come to the Railway Field with us for a while, Robert?'

'Maybe. Sure. I'll go.'

The six of them tagged along to the Railway Field.

Robert was dead-on about Greystones never changing. The road still looked the same.

When they got close to the lane that led into the Railway Field the railway bridge was still in place. And precisely on time the trains would cross the bridge and the narrow sea-eroded cliffs below the Cliff Walk that linked Bray to Greystones.

They went up the laneway, by the pavilion, into their beloved Railway Field.

'Goal.'

'What?'

'I scored a goal there.'

'One goal? You scored about six hundred.'

They stood a while looking at the pitch. The railway line ran on a high embankment to the left. The embankment was wild, untidy, mostly overgrown with brambles and bushes. There were houses directly behind both goals.

Wire netting was spread behind the goals to prevent balls from going into gardens. There were a few other houses too, plus the fire-station and a bungalow-type school just a stone's throw away.

'I outgrew this place two years ago,' gestured Robert Smyth.

'Meanin?'

'I gave up soccer.'

'Maybe you were right to. Soccer isn't your scene.'

That, then, was the Railway Field, with its faded pitch markings, goalposts, trampled goal areas, the pitch lying open, the grass worn and empty, waiting for a player, or players, to place a studded boot on the weary earth and bring the place to life.

The six of them turned and left the Railway Field. They hadn't only left a field. They had left their childhood behind.

They walked under the bridge, went by the harbour, and up the town for a cup of coffee.

Down in the harbour, the sea stirred and blew soft surf on to the stony shore.

The scene looked familiar.

Some places never change.